Rest
Assured

A Salt Mine Novel

Joseph Browning   Suzi Yee

Text Copyright © 2020 by Joseph Browning and Suzi Yee

Published by Expeditious Retreat Press
Cover by J Caleb Design
Edited by Elizabeth VanZwoll

For information regarding Joseph Browning and Suzi Yee's novels and to subscribe to their mailing list, see their website at https://www.joseph-browning.com

To follow them on Twitter: https://twitter.com/Joseph_Browning

To follow Joseph on Facebook: https://www.facebook.com/joseph.browning.52

To follow Suzi on Facebook: https://www.facebook.com/SuziYeeAuthor/

To follow them on MeWe: https://mewe.com/i/josephbrowning

By Joseph Browning and Suzi Yee

THE SALT MINE NOVELS

Money Hungry	Rest Assured
Feeding Frenzy	Hen Pecked
Ground Rules	Brain Drain
Mirror Mirror	Bone Dry
Bottom Line	Vicious Circle
Whip Smart	High Horse

Chapter One

The bountiful berries clung to the tall stalks in the small field of wheat on the side of a low hill. The yield was modest by modern standards, but it was ample to feed the lone man working the edge of the plot. As he bent down and made contact with the golden stalks with his left palm, he instinctually grabbed them like a newborn grasping a finger. Wheat secured, he deftly pulled back his other hand. It comfortably held a well-worn dark knife. His hand knew it well, even if he did not. There was an efficiency to his movements: grab, slash, bundle, drop. Who knew how many times he had repeated this sequence? Certainly not him. He was in a fog, driven by primal forces: eat when hungry, sleep when tired.

As he reached for his next handful, the haze lifted from his brown eyes. For the first time since he'd arrived, he was aware of himself. He released the stalks and raised his gaze from the waves of grain rolling in the soft breeze. Although he couldn't see them, somehow he knew his hill was but one of hundreds stretching out in all directions beneath a cerulean sky dotted with sheep-like clouds. Down slope, tucked between the hills and the apple trees laden with heavy fruit, was a stream that stretched through an intensely green landscape. *As green as… as…* He was searching for words to capture his meaning when he realized that wasn't the only thing missing.

Where am I? Who am I? he puzzled. Out of habit, he checked his watch. The words London, Paris, Cairo, and Moscow leapt out at him from the top of the non-functioning dial. *I know those words. They're places. They mean something. This watch means something.* He briefly stared at the white gold machine, but nothing more came to him.

Unsure of what to do next, he regarded the wheat and watched the cut stalks regrow their dry, golden tops until they were indistinguishable from their unculled neighbors. It didn't strike him as odd, even though he had the feeling it should. The urge to test the phenomena overtook him, and he cut another handful and another. Each time, they too regrew. Somewhere in the doing, it occurred to him that he was hungry. He looked down at the pile he'd made. Suddenly, it made sense to him—*I'm gathering food because I'm hungry!*

He slid his black-bladed knife into the sheath around his waist and was pleased with himself, not just at forming a complete thought but also at having reaped enough wheat. He automatically raised the front of his top and used it as a basket to gather the wheat, which was the first time he gave thought to his clothing. He was dressed in a pair of white samite tunics that descended to mid-thigh, the under chased with blue and gold threads, the upper with gold and purple. A red-leather belt decorated with hunting scenes cinched the fabric around his slim waist, and the end of the belt hung low, weighted by its silver tip. He knew these weren't his clothes, and not just because the well-worn leather shoes were too large for him. They were tied around his calves with what once had been a belt similar to the one he wore around his waist.

The man tucked this nugget of information away with the others he'd just gleaned while he retrieved his harvest. Only after the stalks and berries were secure did he realize he didn't know where to go with his bounty. His temporary moment of indecision passed when he saw a trail of lightly tramped-down grass leading up the hill. *That must be the way I came*, he reasoned as he took the path. The exercise helped clear his brain.

He'd been here forever, but before he'd arrived, he'd been somewhere else. He knew it was true even if it made no sense. I'm used to things that don't make sense, he told himself. A litany bubbled from somewhere deep within him. *I'm the tip of the spear, the edge of the blade, the maker of order from the chaos. I am the fulcrum upon which worlds balance.*

The soft wind broke the rumination and his thoughts lightened. *I'm also rather full of myself, it seems.* He smiled at the insight, only to find the muscles of the face were unaccustomed to such a configuration. Apparently, it wasn't something he did often. He frowned at the realization and found that expression much easier to produce. He made a mental note to rectify that, whoever he was.

When he crested the top of the hill, he knew he'd found the right place. A small windowless rock hut stood next to a large rounded mound atop the center of the hill. It was primitively built, but even at this distance he could see it was solid. Suddenly, he remembered building it and knew things he hadn't yet seen since his fog had lifted. He knew he'd collected many of the stones from the scree along the other side of the hill. He knew he had whittled the wooden door and latch from raw wood with his knife.

But memory felt strange because he saw it from a third person perspective and not from behind his own eyes. Like a camera, he watched himself mortar the stones in place using mud and dried grass. He was wearing different clothes, clothes that he knew had worn out long ago. A precipitous feeling of loss came over him as he understood that everything he'd once had was gone—all except his defunct watch and knife.

He gathered his improvised tunic bag into one hand and drew his knife, looking at it with a more experienced eye. It was thin, half the width it had been when he'd arrived: even the knife was disappearing. His mind went into analysis mode. *How many sharpenings does it take to grind down more than half an inch of…twelve-gauge commercial-grade carbon steel…?* He plucked the words out of his mind. *Thousands? Tens of thousands?* He tried to remember more about the knife, but nothing came.

He sheathed the blade and continued walking toward the hut. The door pulled easily on it rough hinges and the outside light revealed the interior. Farthest from the door, a pile of tunics like the two he wore functioned as a makeshift bed. Opposite the bed was a small fireplace, a diminutive pile of sticks to feed the embers, and a brass jug that he knew contained water. Next to the water jug was a small pile of apples and three stones, two flat-bottomed and one rounded to be held in hand. Tiny flakes of wheat husks liberally dusted the ground. All in all, the hut was less than a hundred square feet, but he knew it kept him warm when the cold came at night.

He entered his humble abode and kept the door open for the light, saving the firewood for cooking and the chilly evening to come. Methodically, he released the berries from the stalk and dropped them on the concave flat-bottomed stone. He wondered how many times he had done this—had the bottom stone always been so concave? Was it the first grinding stone or the latest of many?

With the rounded stone that fit all too well in his hand, he started grinding the wheat, struggling to remember where he'd gotten all the supplies and why all the clothing looked so similar. He poked dark recesses of his mind, trying to awaken the neurons and get them to sync up with the pack. *Great, I remember the word neuron*, he sardonically thought when another memory-vision abruptly came to him.

This time, he was atop a hill, digging into the mound that stood at its center. He wore yet another set of clothing, this one as bare and thin as he was. Using a long stick, he levered large stones out of the way and revealed an entrance. Inside, light from a single candle danced in the air, feeding off nothing and hovering over an ornately carved bier upon which lay a fresh-looking corpse, clad in finest samite. As he approached, the dancing candle seemed to bow toward him.

They're all tombs! he triumphantly thought as he pieced together the true nature of the endless hills around him. Then, an erudite voice corrected him, *Actually, they are tumuli.* He rued his stream of consciousness—*I can't remember who I am, but I know the difference between a tomb and a tumulus?* As if to spite him, his mind filled in the blanks. *I'm...I'm...David Emrys Wilson and I'm in Avalon.*

Avalon: land of the fallen warrior, home to the dead who had spent their life fighting against chaos or evil or both. It was an unassailable refuge from both the living and the dead. The living couldn't enter and the dead were stripped of their freewill once they stepped upon the hallowed shores, lest they disturb their neighbors. Avalon was a well-earned rest, a quiet place where every day was a year in miniature, that began with the first blush of spring and ended with winter's arrival.

He reflexively shivered as the recollection of all the cold evenings he'd spent rough before he built the stone hut. He'd huddled in grass and whatever debris he could find to keep himself warm, loading up on as much food during the autumnal afternoons to survive the wintry nights. Once he figured out the mounds were tombs, he'd raided them for supplies and the large flat rocks that formed the foundation of his hut; his primal monkey-mind hadn't allowed him to sleep with the dead.

His new home didn't have a door at first, but shelter with a fire and a surplus of tunics stripped off the eternally fresh dead was so blissful, it had brought tears to his senseless eyes. It didn't take long for him to fashion a door; even in his fugue, something insisted on having a physical barrier between his space and the rest of Avalon. Houses had doors. At least the safe ones did.

Wilson checked the coarseness of the ground meal and deemed it sufficient. Using the dry wheat stalks, he kindled a spark with a hand drill fire-starting stick and lit the fire, laying the second flat stone over the flames once he was certain it had caught. His hands then returned to the flour, shaping it into a mound before creating a well in the center. He reached for the brass jug and paused to appreciate the battle scenes etched into its side with late-medieval ornamentation. He tipped it sideways but stopped before drizzling the water into the flour. I'm in Avalon—*I should check to make sure the water's safe.* The notion niggled at him as he tried to decipher its full meaning. He thought hard. *Think, think, think...*

"I'm a magician!" he said aloud, almost dropping the water

jug. His throat was rough and rusty. Who knew how long it was since he last said anything? He smiled broadly, not just because the water wasn't magical, but because he recognized his voice as his own. He didn't know why he found that so immensely comforting, but he did.

His stomach growled at him, and he resumed making his dinner. He incorporated the water and kneaded it into a rough dough that made a passable unleavened bread once it was cooked on the heated stone. Hunger was the best sauce, but what he wouldn't do for a little salt. He laughed out loud without knowing why that was so funny, and the sound of his chuckle bounced off the rock walls.

Wilson closed and latched the door while the first piece of bread cooked. A flood of information became accessible once he rediscovered the basics of casting, and his mind chewed on his circumstances because nothing made sense. By all rights, he shouldn't be here because Avalon only accepted the dead and he was very much alive. *How on earth did I get here?*

His mind ran down everything he knew about Avalon, most of which was derived from variants of the Arthurian legend. It was ruled by a power named Viviane, in council with her eight sisters. It was the forge source of Excalibur and its waters were reputed to have healing properties. He stared at his brass jug and sighed. "I guess that one is bunk," he spoke, getting use to talking again, even if it was to himself. Still, he'd have to check the stream tomorrow—enchanted water had a habit of losing its magic when taken from its source.

Then another thought crossed his mind. *If there are tombs, where are the tomb builders?* The more he remembered, the more angles he had to cover and the list of unanswered questions grew even longer. It took the smell of the bread to bring him back to the present.

As soon as the uncooked side started bubbling, he flipped the flat bread with a makeshift pair of chopsticks and let the other side cook. The second side always took less time than the first, and his mouth watered at the thought of food. He let the first piece cool as he put another on the heated stone over the fire. Wilson devoured the bread as he watched the coals underneath the fresh wood burn bright red. It was mesmerizing and reminded him of something he couldn't put his finger on.

Fueled by a little food, he pressed his mind to make a connection until he had a name—*Baba Yaga*. The words burned into his brain, and it unlocked a whole cache of memories. Yes, Wilson remembered everything now, and he edged closer to the fire for warmth and light.

Chapter Two

Wilson awoke with the dawn of spring, nestled in the mound of tunics that served as his bed and blanket. There were no alarms, bird songs, or buzzing insects to herald the emergence of a new day-slash-season. Avalon was a silent kingdom, and Wilson was pretty sure he was the only living thing among the hills, save the plants. Upon reflection, he realized that he'd never even uncovered a single worm or grub while digging out the tombs.

Wilson checked in with his brain and found all the memories recovered yesterday were still in place. In what felt like the past month to him, he had found out Alex was still alive, was shunted into a time loop by a time elemental, summoned Poseidon, and struck a bargain with Baba Yaga…which obviously went pear-shaped somewhere, because his original plan definitely didn't end in Avalon. Before he'd retired last night, Wilson had made himself a promise—if his reawaking took, tomorrow was going to be the first day of the rest of his life. Even sleep was a leap of faith in Avalon.

Despite everything, he felt good this morning. He felt

more himself than he had in ages, and for the first time in who knows how long, he had a plan. Today was a new beginning. Today was wash day. His return to cognizance had brought to light the terrible state of uncleanliness, both of his person and his abode. His primal subconscious may have provided water, food, and shelter, but it was sorely deficient in personal hygiene. Put quite simply, he was filthy and wearing clothes stolen from dead people.

He pushed off the layers of makeshift bedding and launched himself into the day with gusto. Breakfast was three apples eaten in rapid succession, and he added some wood to the dwindled fire before setting off. He opened the door and threw out the apple cores, which would rot with such rapidity that he wouldn't be able to find them tomorrow. It was one of the quirks of Avalon he was able to enumerate last night—things existed here because they had purpose and their existence was utterly dedicated to that function. Take the apples. Wilson could pick an apple and it would stay fresh forever in its little pile near the water jug. But if he decided he didn't want it and threw it out, it would rot within a day.

He wasn't certain what his purpose had been in his primal state, but now that he was fully conscious, he made an iron-willed goal to ensure he would not rot like a discarded apple core—he would escape Avalon. He didn't know exactly *how* he was going to get out, but he had a gut feeling it wasn't going to be easy. Thus, his scheme started with cleaning up. An elephant wasn't eaten in one bite.

In Wilson-like fashion, he assessed his resources. Avalon was accommodating to a point, but it wasn't like there was a tree that fruited soap, a bush that sprouted combs and razors, or a stand of brooms that grew along the stream. He'd been in enough tombs to know the standard fare found within, and his first target would be more brass jugs for the larger campaign of soap making, which required lye, fat, and a heat source. He'd been burning applewood in his hut, and extracting lye from hardwood ashes was a simple matter of boiling the ashes in water and skimming the liquid lye off the top. The tricky part was the requisite fat required for saponification. There were no animals to kill for meat, much less fat, and he didn't remember seeing any olive or avocado trees in Avalon. Still, saving the ashes was a step forward, and any progress was welcomed this early in the game.

He left the hut and headed toward the nearest tomb. It felt strange leaving "home" without locking the door, even though there wasn't a need. Now that he was fully self-aware, he defaulted to his standard MO, sending out his will for magical traps before crawling over the rocky entrance and into the tomb. It was cross-shaped with the now-naked corpse at the tip. A single candle flame flickered and bobbed over the body with brass, copper, silver, and gold grave goods in the wings. He grabbed suitable containers and made his way back to the hut. A dirty ten minutes later, he had all the ashes he'd need tucked away in the corner with empty pots to spare.

As soon as he had a broom, he could give the fireplace, along with the rest of the hut, a good sweeping. Unfortunately, it would be hours before the wheat even sprouted, and he didn't want to waste his day waiting for time to pass. He had done enough of that in his fugue state. Undeterred he made his way to the nearby stream; if he could dam it, it would make a decent wash basin that was constantly circulating clean water. If he could get it deep enough, he could even take a proper bath. Plus, he wanted to know if the waters of Avalon were, in fact, enchanted.

His feet knew well the path to the stream, trod many times in their oversized shoes. Everything was the same as in preceding days, except that Wilson was himself again. The familiar bucolic landscape held new possibilities when observed in his perception. The gurgling pristine water looked inviting, but he ran his will over it before filling his jug to make sure everything was as it seemed. Much to his disappointment, the water wasn't magical, but he was gladdened to note the lack of euphoria that typically came when he performed certain types of magic on Earth. Whatever Avalon was, it played by its own rules. The only other place he could cast without that annoying side effect was the Magh Meall, and this was definitely not the middle lands.

Satisfied with the state of the water, he walked upstream and found a precipitous drop in elevation that would allow some depth if he dammed directly downstream. Using a mix of nearby stones and some pilfered from the four closest tombs, he engineered a water pool roughly a foot and a half deep. In his estimation, he could maybe get another six inches but it would take significantly more effort and stone. Every inch upward increased the width of the stream's surface, which meant even more stone. He'd spent all morning to get this far, and he was content to test what he had already built before committing to more.

His stomach growled, and he crossed the stream and trekked toward to the apple orchard for lunch. A cluster of majestic apple trees stood on the low slope of the hill, the tallest nearing twenty-five feet. The trees always ripened before the wheat, and just as with the grain, a perfectly ripe apple regrew as soon as he plucked one from the tree. As the weather warmed, he sated his thirst and hunger in the shade of one of the trees.

After eating, Wilson stretched his legs and climbed to the top of the closest tumulus for some scouting. As he stood at its top, he did the math—given the height of the hill and his personal height, he could see approximately three miles. He did a full circle and there were gentle rolling hills, each topped with their own tumulus, on all sides for as far as he could see. Sadly, there was no way to tell which direction was more promising than the others. Wilson made an assumption and named where the sun rose "east" and where it set "west." It wasn't the same as on Earth, but it would do for lack of a better nomenclature.

Of all the directions to go, he could only rule out west. He'd come from that direction. After he'd clawed his way out of his tomb, he'd traveled for days before eventually stopping and building the hut. There wasn't anything back there but more of the same.

Normally, he would just follow one of the streams to the sea, as Avalon was an island and most island streams eventually lead to an ocean. The problem, of course, was that Avalon didn't adhere to the rules of rational topography—where the streams hit a low point, the water simply drained away, as if flowing into underground caverns.

What he really needed was more height, but all the hilltops were bare. *Unless...* Wilson pulled out his knife and cut one of the apples in half, exposing the cluster of seeds. He dug into the ground and loosened the dirt before dropping in and covering a seed with soil. He lightly watered it and consciously stated his desire for it to grow.

He didn't know how mutable Avalon was to his consciousness, but it was worth a shot. Apple trees grew up to thirty feet, and if he could get that kind of elevation on top of a mound, he could see five to six times farther. It would save him a lot of time spent walking. In his primal state, growing his own apple tree would have never crossed his mind when he had a slew of mature apple trees with regenerating fruit.

He ran the numbers on his journey back to the stream via the apple orchard to pick a few more for later consumption. If a day in Avalon is a year in miniature, how long would it take an apple tree to grow to maturity? Would it be a sapling this time tomorrow? He made a mental note to start hash marking the days on one of the stones in his hut to keep track of the tree's growth and his conscious time in Avalon. Good records were vital to making optimal decisions.

It was the height of summer when he crossed back over the stream, and the cool water seemed refreshing instead of bracing. Wilson talked himself into taking a dip in his shallow pool—what better way to test it? He may not have soap, but he could mechanically scrub off the grime on his skin, head, and hair and give his two tunics some semblance of cleaning while still having enough time for them to dry before it cooled off.

Wilson unbuckled the leather straps that kept his shoes secured, placing his footwear far enough from the water that they wouldn't get wet. He took his outer tunic off and beat it against a rock, getting as much dust and dry dirt off as possible before plunging it into the pool. He agitated the submerged garment, rubbing one part against another to shake loose the grime that had collected. He would have liked soap, but at least it certainly smelled better coming out than it did going in. He wrung it dry before laying it out in full sun.

Then, he took his inner tunic off and set it aside, just in case his clean tunic wasn't dry before autumn came. He knew he had to have been naked before to change his worn-out tunics, but it was the first time since his return to cognizance that he'd gotten a good look at himself. He didn't recognize the reflection in the rippling water as he approached the pool. He was far thinner than he remembered being, and his hair much longer than he'd ever worn it. His beard was bushy and wild, but it couldn't hide the lean gauntness underneath.

Wilson slid into the pool, and the water came up to his knees. He bent down to submerge as much of his body as he could. He used his hands to scrub away the dirt from his face and beard, then his hair, and last his body. In the course of washing, he found himself touching his left side. There used to be massive scars running from his back to abdomen—a souvenir from the karakura mauling he'd endured in that faraway Japanese coalmine. It was bad enough that "bear attack" had been his story whenever asked. Except now, it was gone. He'd grown accustomed to the rough ridges with their nearly Plasticine feel, and the tightness he felt when he twisted to the right. It felt weird now that the physical scars were gone, because he still had all the unseen ones.

Well, not all, he mused as he rubbed under his pits. *Baba Yaga kept her end of the bargain.* Wilson had known it was a risky gambit, but he hadn't been left with very many options once he realized he wasn't a whole person and never could be. Wilson would always be grateful that Alex had saved his life in Utashinai, even though it had left him less than his full self; neither of them could have known what it would do to Wilson's soul.

Every human—as well as some other creatures—had a soul. It was what devils and demons wanted from humans—their motive force, their spark of transient life that, once freed of the body, could be coerced by the powerful to survive indefinitely. Souls were tough; they bounced back from deep injuries, slowly regrowing from the deepest wounds. A person could easily lose more than half their soul and keep going. Wilson had once, in an encounter with a vampire, and it had grown back within a month.

The problem with the shadow demon attack was that Wilson's body had been so damaged his soul had willingly left. It wasn't damaged, it was absent. Somehow, Alex had reached into the Land of the Dead and pulled back the shreds that remained and stitched them together with part of his own, leaving Wilson alive, but hollowed. For years, he'd felt that there was always an echo within. His soul would never regrow because it had no space to grow into, and the new parts didn't quite fit right. It was like a metaphysical transplant rejection. Once he'd accepted that he wasn't a whole person and never could be in his current state, the risk assessment changed and the dangers of trying to set things right became acceptable.

Wilson was, more than anything, a private man. His dealings were his alone. That was how he'd decided upon Baba Yaga. She was an ancient power, one that could be bargained with and, most importantly, one that would never speak to anyone that Wilson knew. Leader, Chloe and Dot, Alex, none of them would deal with Baba Yaga. Devils, demons, fae? Yes, but never the ancient Russian Witch of the Forest. Only crazy people willingly dealt with her.

He had all his affairs in order, both mundane and magical, just in case things didn't go according to plan. Just before he'd crossed into the Magh Meall, he'd sent off a quick email to Leader, knowing she'd tell those who needed to know what they needed to hear. As much as he valued his privacy, he felt like he owed them an explanation if he didn't come back.

Wilson shivered as he recalled the mobile shack running toward him on giant chicken legs, and left his pool. He wasn't clean, but he was noticeably less dirty. He lay on a patch of soft grass and dried off in the late summer sun, thankful that he wasn't infested with vermin due to Avalon's unique nature. The old Wilson would have tutted the lack of cover and the absence of sunscreen, but the new Wilson was not bothered. He wouldn't be more than a few minutes, and there was still the wheat to harvest and straw to make the broom.

The rays beat down and he closed his eyes, replaying the exchange with the witch and how it had gone wrong. Baba Yaga had been surprised by the offer. It wasn't every day a human approached with the rare and treasured gift of the scales of a charmed fish. And all they wanted in exchange was for you to tear their soul apart? Unheard of! He remembered her coal-like eyes, both fiery and rheumy at the same time, darting around her chicken-legged hut as if to visually find the trap in the deal.

Eventually, cautiously, she'd agreed.

Had everything gone to plan, Wilson would have woken up somewhere in the Magh Meall with much less soul, but all of it his. But he didn't. He'd woken up here, meaning that he'd died. Which he could accept...but if he was dead, why could he feel the sliver of his soul regrowing? And since the living couldn't enter Avalon, what was going to happen when it reached one hundred percent?

Wilson rose and dressed, slinging his clean-but-still-damp tunic over his shoulder. His gut warned him he was on the clock, and he had miles to go before he slept.

Chapter Three

Morning brought spring as it always did, but today, Wilson rose without eating and walked to the top of the neighboring tumulus to check on the apple seed he'd planted yesterday. A boyish enthusiasm propelled him over the stream, through the orchard, and up the slope. Avalon was supposed to be void of living or free-willed beings, and yet it had tended to his basic needs in his fugue state. Now that he was cognizant again, would it bend to his stated will?

Even before he reached the top of the mound, Wilson had his answer—a small sapling that came waist high when he measured it against himself. He gleefully smiled; at this rate, it would reach maturity in about ten days. As long as the tree was scalable, he could survey at least twenty-five times more area at those heights. He patted the young tree with a stoic "that will do, pig" and was slightly disappointed that no one was there to laugh at his joke.

He took a calculated risk and poured a little magic into the soil to see if he could expedite its growth. Avalon was an enchanted place, like the Magh Meall, and he reasoned that it too might also bypass the karmic costs associated with magic on Earth. He could always revisit his stance if he suddenly started stubbing his toe more often or having more small mishaps, but if raiding tombs in a magical cemetery wasn't enough to damn him, he was pretty sure he was out of karma's reach. At least, he hoped so. There would be no way for him to offset karmic debt as the only living creature in a mythic cemetery. If he accrued it, he would pay for it the hard way.

He headed back to his hut for breakfast, filling two brass jugs of water in the stream on the way. In his primal state, he did what he needed to do to survive, but now that he had regained his mental faculties, he had the ability to optimize and thrive. For example, he'd gathered excess wheat yesterday and cooked extra bread so he would have more to eat this morning. Using the tunic for warmth was a given, but only now could he think to repurpose the pile of excess leather belts into straps and ties to make it easier to carry more on his ventures to the wheat field, stream, and orchard. Fire was essential to cooking bread and keeping warm in his fugue state, but it also made light, and last night he'd made the most of it, whittling the beginnings of a handle for a broom while he waited for each flat loaf to cook.

He devoured cold bread and a couple of apples before completing the broom from last night. Essentially, he was aiming for something that resembled a napkin holder through which he could thread as much straw as possible. That way, he could replace the straw regularly but reuse the wooden ring. The result was short and primitive, but it worked.

Wilson moved his gear outside of the hut, determined to give the entire hut the spring cleaning it needed. First, he swept dust and debris out with his new broom. Once he had his first cleanish spot, it was pretty obvious how bad things had gotten. He splashed water on the floor and followed each round with vigorous swipes of the broom. Eventually, the water running out his door was almost clear.

His plan was to leave the door open to let everything dry out while he washed his bedding tunics. It was only late spring, giving them all of summer to dry if he got moving. While his gut didn't like leaving everything out and open, he knew there was no reason to fear his things sitting outside—it never rained in Avalon, and it wasn't like anyone was going to take anything.

He propped the broom against the side of the hut and started bundling tunics with a leather strap when he caught a shadow in his peripheral vision. His instinct and training kicked in and without turning his head, he dropped the tunics and drew his knife, twisting and crouching in a single motion. His keen eyes quickly found the source of the shadow—atop the tumulus stood a massive apple tree growing at speeds observable by the human eye. Its limbs burst out of its sides and leafed at such velocity, it was like watching sped-up time-lapse footage.

"Woah," he said aloud, stunned at the display. He sheathed his knife and left his plans of laundry to visit the newly arisen tree. He guessed it was more than thirty feet tall, large for an apple tree, and the limbs jutted out at convenient intervals, almost as if it was made to be scaled. *Which it was*, he thought to himself as he started climbing.

His victorious mood was quickly tempered when he saw the view from the top—an endless repetition of hills with tumuli in all directions. It was like someone took a stamp and reproduced the same vignette over and over again, down to the stream between hills with a wheat field on one side and an orchard on the other. The wind was bracing at such a height, but it helped him think. Notions of cleaning and homesteading were replaced by thoughts of mobility and travel.

The good news was that he could grow a viewing perch wherever he wanted one, allowing him to pick a direction and still be able to scout out the surrounding area as he went. He would have all the same raw materials during his travel, and he could mobile in a day. His hindbrain decried sleeping rough again, but Wilson was no longer in his fugue state. He knew what was coming and could take preemptive measures. If there was a *somewhere* he could go to get out of Avalon, it wasn't here. And his growing soul kept telling him it was imperative to get out.

*****

According to the hash marks on his leather belt, it had been eleven days since Wilson had left his little stone hut and walked east into the rising sun. The journey had been relentlessly repetitious, both in scenery and activity. His pace was rigorous, marching through the entire day from sunup to mid-autumn, often taking food and water on foot. Based on the fact that he could barely see the prior day's tree, he guessed he was traveling close to thirty miles each day he traveled. Once he reached a stopping point, he would climb to the top of the next hill and plant a seed before winter could set in. He'd left a trail of large apple trees behind him, like breadcrumbs should he ever have to backtrack.

The remainder of the day would be spent growing the tree, scouting, harvesting more wheat, making more bread, and collecting plenty of wood for a roaring fire. The nights were cold but tolerable, thanks to his makeshift kit and the fact that he used heated flat stones during the night, an enhanced survival tactic he couldn't have tried in his primal state. He'd spent more than a night at a single location only once—to dig into a mound and replenish his supplies. Even the mounds were the same, except each contained a unique corpse.

The exercise and discipline of routine had done him good. He felt more like himself with each passing day, and even started to fill out again once he forced himself to eat more than he really cared to and had restarted his daily calisthenics. It would have gone faster with protein, but excess calories was a start.

The morning of the twelfth day started like the prior, and Wilson climbed his latest apple tree atop a hill. He took more care as his shoes gripped the bark—he was breaking in a new pair of shoes, liberated from the last mound he'd raided. They were oversized, but that was something proper strapping could address. Undersized shoes were worthless.

Once he was secure, he looked to the east and saw something novel and new—a giant swath of deep blue ringed the horizon far over the hills. The spike of adrenaline from the climb heightened his elation—*Avalon does have a shore!* His brain raced with all the things he needed to do even as he carefully descended. All the stories described Avalon as an island, and it looked like he'd finally reached its end.

It wasn't until he was back at his camp in the lee of the hill, stuffing his face with apples and yesterday's bread, that his enthusiasm waned. He had no idea what he would encounter on the coast. Would it be wild and uninhabited, or would there be other intelligent life? By this point, Wilson was pretty sure he was an anomaly, a corner case, a statistical outlier. If there was life native to Avalon—tomb builders, if you will—what form would they take? How would they respond to him—a mortal that by all appearances had returned from the dead?

Not for the first time, he wished he had his phone and the library of information he kept on it. Or better yet, access to Chloe and Dot, the Salt Mine's resident librarians. Wilson's knowledge of Avalon was disturbingly small, and he was certain most of it was bunk, worthless information gleaned from tertiary—or worse, *cultural*—sources.

He secured his pack, grabbed his walking stick, and climbed over the first of many more hills. If he pushed, he would reach the shore by late summer, which would give him more daylight to adapt to whatever he discovered. His natural caution percolated through as he trekked, and he started paying closer attention to his surroundings around late spring. He was the first to admit he'd grown complacent over the days, since everything was the same as what had come before. *Repetition breeds carelessness.*

It wasn't long after lunch that the first whiff of salty ocean air drifted over the hills. Wilson slowed his advance and carefully approached the next hill. He dropped his pack at the edge of the tumulus and crawled up to minimize his profile. He barely popped his head over the top, just enough to get eyes on where the sea met land.

A stone pier jutted out from a long sandy beach, and docked upon it was a long sailing ship—a carrack, if he wasn't mistaken. It was being unloaded by bipedal creatures of the likes he had never seen before. At one moment, they looked perfectly human, but the next, they were tall and thin with elongated arms, legs, and necks that ended in rounded featureless fleshy balls. They flickered between the two states, like a movie reel with every other frame sliced with their alternate form.

They were unloading coffins off the vessel—undecorated

solid black things without any apparent identification marks, at least none that he could see at this distance. He needed to get closer. He ducked down, retrieved his pack, and belly-crawled over the hill, down into the valley and then repeated the maneuver a dozen more times, each time pausing to see more until he finally arrived at the last hill ridge. During the process, two ships, a galleon and a caravel, had arrived and unloaded before returning to the open water.

From his final vantage point, he saw a narrow cobbled road running parallel to the shore as far as he could see. On the west side of the paved path stood a series of stone buildings with lightly sloped and slated roofs. The blinkers—as he had come to call the flickering creatures—transported each of the coffins off the vessels into one of these structures. They moved with coordinated efficiency, and if they were communicating with each other, Wilson couldn't tell. There were no yells, flashing lights, or overt gestures—just bodies in synchronized motion.

Another ship—this time a junk with majestic red sails— arrived, and Wilson was close enough to see there was no crew manning the vessel. It simply did what needed to happen; ropes coiled, sails moved, rudders turned, all of their own volition. The blinkers met it at the pier and started transporting more black coffins into the warehouses, but this time Wilson was close enough to see their human likeness changed with each coffin. They were all Asian, but distinctly unique. *Could they be taking the form of the body within?* he speculated to himself as a blinker carried the last coffin off the ship. The self-operating vessel immediately set sail.

Unlike the other coffins, the last wasn't taken into one of the stone buildings. The blinker bearing it brought it to the thin cobbled road and placed it on the green grass on the opposite side of the buildings. Then, the cadre of blinkers proceeded to empty the warehouses of the coffins they had just placed within. Wilson counted as the black boxes lined up next to each other, one hundred coffins lying precisely perpendicular to the road.

The twenty blinkers congregated and raised their arms, flickering between their elongated forms and that of a beautiful woman. They then broke into song, a forty-part harmony that certainly would have been impossible in the mortal realm. The sound hit Wilson like a physical force, and before he knew what he was doing, he stood up on the mound and added his voice to their song. He mourned those that had passed, and paid homage to the one hundred stories that lay before him— souls that had held back the forces of evil. He recounted their successes and losses, their beginnings and ends.

Wilson didn't know *how* he knew the words, only that they must be sung for the fallen. He was one with the song, and the song was with Avalon. As the verse finished the tale of a life, the bodies were placed into their newly created tombs throughout Avalon, and he traveled the depth and breadth of the island one hundred times over. He learned of Avalon itself, how everything related to its center point and first tomb—the tomb of King Arthur.

When the final chorus was sung and the spell ended, Wilson felt heavy and spent, like those first few steps taken on dry land after a long swim at sea. His wobbly legs barely held as he remained standing; there wasn't a point of hiding after he had already joined their choir. He waited for the blinkers to react to his presence, but they were indifferent to him. Either they didn't see him or they didn't care. He considered directly hailing them but changed his mind when they started dismantling the coffins and eating them.

Chapter Four

The Valley of the Magi
Somewhere in Time

Hor-Nebwy casually expressed his will, refilling the simple clay lamp with oil. The flame at the end of the rolled linen wick momentarily sputtered and then resumed steadily illuminating the solid wall of rock. He worked through the disruption in light, fully engrossed in his task of etching the final hieroglyph onto the sandstone. He had long ago lost his mundane sight and didn't technically need the lamp to see, but he kept it lit by his side nonetheless. It was tradition.

His crouched emaciated form cast a long, thin shadow across the tomb as he drew each symbol with precision. The tomb was one of his many works in progress: a quarter was finished and painted in painstaking detail, half was still in the carving process, and with a final stroke of his chalk, the final quarter was finally drawn upon the walls. It now awaited the mason's tools to bring the art into the third dimension. Hor-Nebwy did all of the work to his own demanding expectations. He produced only the best every time.

He had no guide next to him, nor was there a more-experienced caretaker informing his work. There was no tome held open to the final pages from which to mimic. Hor-Nebwy crafted from memory—a consciousness that had been making such inscriptions for millennia. Were any of the pernicious human diggers witness to his creation, they would say he'd worked from *The Book of the Dead*. They would never suspect that, in fact, he was the one responsible for the perfection of that complement of spells that gave the dead good service in the afterlife. To Hor-Nebwy, they were simply his spells.

His skin crackled as he rose to his full height, carefully lifting the small lamp with him. He rested a dry, gray hand upon the center sarcophagus that he'd cut from the rock itself. It too was covered in ornate, chalk-drawn images. He always enjoyed the feel of the stone. It gave the impression of being invulnerable, but it always bent to his will. A feeling of satisfaction washed over him—there was a place for everything and everything was in its place. He would have stayed and worked longer, but it was almost time for prayers, and Hor-Nebwy loathed tardiness. It was against his nature.

He blew out the lamp and gracefully passed through three long halls before exiting the tomb. The blazing heat greeted him as he stepped onto the canyon floor at the mouth of the rocky ridge that gave way to an endless sea of sand. Across the shoulders of the valley, hundreds of other tombs—most occupied, several in progress—dotted the cliffs. Their rectangular black mouths were sprinkled across the tan stone with increasing frequency the nearer to the valley floor. A crass person would have called them the "cheap seats," but Hor-Nebwy didn't think like that. He knew there was an order within all things and finding that order brought a resonate peace. That was what Hor-Nebwy created: a serenity that vibrated through to the afterlife. He raised his eyes higher and admired his work. In the Valley of the Magi, silence reigned and nothing could be heard moving but sand in the wind.

The sun bore down with all its might as Hor-Nebwy knelt on the sand. With the lamp placed beside him, he raised his arms to the sky in praise. His parched voice broke the silence as it did every day at noon and the valley filled with the ancient song of the last true priest of Horus. It wasn't an invocation of kingship, full of bluster and entitlement by divine right, nor was it the sweet melodious chorus sung by women and children: it was a raspy benediction from one ancient being to another, albeit a much more puissant one. There was respect and resignation in the cracks and gravelly tones. It was done because that's what one did when they dedicated their life and afterlife to The One Who Is Above.

His singing attracted the attention of the two serpopard guardians that constantly patrolled the mouth of the valley. Their leopard bodies slinked across the sand with silent feline agility, and their elongated necks serpentined before them. They nudged their furry heads against Hor-Nebwy as he prayed. He absentmindedly scratched behind their ears without disruption to his song. He could go weeks without seeing them, but they were always affectionate when their paths crossed. They hung around, waiting for him to produce any treats he may have hidden in his wrappings, but once it was obvious none were forthcoming, the serpopards tired of his companionship and returned to the sand just before he finished his prayers.

Silence descended upon the valley once more as he gathered his lamp, rose from the sands, and started the long trek to the temple in the middle of the valley. Every month, he had to perform the rituals that hid the valley from prying eyes as well as the rites that kept the valley in a reality adjacent to the one in which he'd been born. Tomorrow would be a busy day, and the priest had to ready himself.

The tops of the temple's tall pillars had just come into view when he felt the first tingle of a contact: someone wanted to speak with him. He wasn't entirely surprised by the petition; among certain esoteric circles, Hor-Nebwy was an institution. To have him agree to take care of a practitioner's afterlife was a great honor because he was selective in whom he interred in the Valley of the Magi.

As an old power, he was unmoved by trivial things. He couldn't be bought by money or swayed by reputation. He judged applicants by their worthiness, and he had come across enough mortal casters to intuit the difference between the sincere and powerful and the counterfeit or weak. He rarely answered the pleas of the former and ignored the latter completely. Of course, those who genuinely understood the importance of his work were given extra consideration.

The priest paused and let the electric sensation roll over him. It always started in his extremities and worked its way to the center of his forehead. The tingle had only reached his ankles and wrists when he realized this request was something different. Something new.

As a general rule, Hor-Nebwy didn't care for the new, but different perked his interest. It was rare to come across novel things when one had existed as long as he had. He let himself drift out of his body and into the summoning circle of the petitioner.

"I am here," Hor-Nebwy solemnly announced his arrival. His senses perceived the simple brass circle cast directly into the ground. A running collection of hieroglyphs were inscribed upon the circle, many of which contained errors. Whoever had summoned him had only a passible understanding of Hor-Nebwy's mother tongue. The writing had been just accurate enough to draw his attention, but the priest was certain that it would not contain him if he chose to leave.

"I welcome you here," Wilson prostrated himself. Hor-Nebwy looked past the long filthy beard and the dirty pair of tunics that clothed him, and saw the honest desperation in the seeker's countenance. To Hor-Nebwy's preternatural eyes, the creature in front of him was a being of life—one that glowed in pulsating whites with such intensity that he found it difficult to look directly at him.

He turned his gaze on their surroundings, taking in the vast field of hills, each topped with a primitive tomb. He immediately recognized the environs, except that it was impossible for him to be here—he knew the place was distinctly warded against him.

"How am I in Avalon?" he demanded. "How have you breached the wards?"

"No wards have been broken," Wilson respectfully answered. "You and I are here according to all the inscribed laws. I am merely a loophole. Your vision will reveal the truth."

Hor-Nebwy forced his necromantic eyes to dive into the luminous being before him. He pierced through the glowing shell of life and only then did he find an interior of death, the dim place of silence and solitude.

"You are both alive and dead," he stated incredulously. "How is that possible?"

Wilson pulsed more of his life force into the connection and graciously replied, "I would love to tell you the full story, but I fear I have very little time." Hor-Nebwy saw he was telling the truth; every second, the light of life was burning away and the glowing shell becoming thinner. The magician was burning his own soul to feed the summoning. That in and of itself took incredible will and discipline. "Soon I will fade and lose all will and become nothing more than a mindless body wandering these hills forever. And when I fade, your chance fades with me."

"Chance of what?" Hor-Nebwy inquired curiously. He was accustomed to people asking for things, but this being wanted to make a deal.

"Your chance to claim this for your realm," Wilson said, waving his arms over his pack and toward the wrapped body at his side. He rose and carefully removed the cloth from its face.

"Arthur!" Hor-Nebwy exclaimed.

"And Excalibur," Wilson said, revealing the ivory and gold hilt of the sword tucked into his filthy pack.

Hor-Nebwy didn't hesitate, "What do you want me to do?"

"I want you to give me temporary dominion over Mau so that I can order her to retrieve me from here and lead me back to my world," Wilson spoke plainly but rapidly. He could feel the fringes of his soul starting to unravel.

"That is impossible," Hor-Nebwy scoffed. "She cannot enter Avalon."

"Yes she can," Wilson gently corrected him, carefully controlling each syllable as the weight of the summoning bore down upon him. "If I have dominion over her, she is acting as the materialization of my will and can go anywhere that I can go. I am not of Avalon and yet I am here: the wards will not prevent her entry or exit in the retrieval process any more than they are affecting me. Avalon only guards what belongs to Avalon."

Hor-Nebwy's dry eyes narrowed reflexively, even though they were no longer the seat of his vision. "And why cannot you leave of your own power?"

"I am but human. I don't have the power. Mau is greater than me," Wilson uttered, exhausted.

Hor-Nebwy nodded at the direct response. "And in exchange, you provide me the body and sword of Arthur and the return of Mau when you have returned?"

"I will bring them with me when I leave. The things I carry are mine and not bound here, and Mau will always be yours," Wilson reassured him.

Hor-Nebwy looked closely at the man, now shaking with the strain of the summons, and watched his life burning away. The soot of his soul drifted behind him in the gentle wind. The priest preferred time to contemplate the potential ramifications, but he had little time to entertain the offer. Soon, the man would unable to maintain the contact and the opportunity would be gone.

"Agreed," he declared, and recited the words of obligation. "I am bound to do what you desire and you are bound to do what I desire."

Wilson felt the power in Hor-Nebwy's words and flashed a bright smile made more brilliant in contrast to his darkening face. "Agreed. We are mutually bound," he voiced the appropriate reply. "I now exercise my will. Mau, I order you to bring me from Avalon and return me to Detroit!" Hor-Nebwy was blinded by the intense flash as Wilson burned more of his soul to seal the deal and make his will known across the realms.

When his vision cleared, the rolling hills of Avalon were gone. He was back in his desert domain and he moved with unaccustomed speed to the head of the Valley of the Magi. Mau resided in the first tomb he'd built in the valley, high up on the farthest hill. He hadn't been in that part of the valley in years, but his steps never hesitated or faltered, for Mau was a resident of Hor-Nebwy's personal tomb.

It was a surprisingly modest affair, a single decorated corridor sloping gently to twin chambers adorned in similar fashion. The first contained his grave goods while the second held his sarcophagus and a low cedar chest that secured his canopic jars. Atop the canopic chest, his mummified cat Mau lay, still curled in sleep after so many years.

"Mau, I am in need of your service," he heavily intoned as he transferred the cat to the top of his sarcophagus. Hor-Nebwy waited as his sepulchral voice traveled beyond the veil between the living and the dead. Wherever Mau had gotten to, she would soon hear and answer her master.

"Mau, I am in need of your service," he repeated himself after a few minutes. His heard his will echo through the realms, but his cat remained still.

Hor-Nebwy knew something was wrong. Mau could be stubborn and fickle as any living cat, but to not answer her master after a second call was unheard of. He turned his preternatural gaze upon Mau and roared with indignation at his discovery—someone had stolen his beloved and replaced it with a poorly mummified double!

Chapter Five

Detroit, Michigan, USA
13th of October, 11:07 p.m. (GMT-4)

The dimly lit promenade of the Detroit Institute of Arts was silent, save the low rumble of the janitor's cart as it rolled past the Prentis Court and turned into the Romanesque Hall. The wheels squeaked as it stopped on the interlocking gray tiles; the sound bounced off the high ceilings and echoed throughout the halls. Isaiah Dufrane grabbed his mop and got to work.

There was a cadence to his mopping—swish, swish, swish, wring, dunk, wring, swish, swish, swish. Some might have thought it monotonous or tedious, but not Dufrane. He found it meditative. Some nights, he would become lost in the movement and find he'd cleaned half a building without really thinking about it. He patted the stone lion as he passed its section of the room, his way of greeting the familiar form that helped orient his route.

Dufrane had spent most of his life as a janitor, and he couldn't imagine doing anything else. It wasn't like he'd planned for this to be his career, but he didn't have very many options after he served a short stint in prison for a casual but unwise association with a street gang during his youth. Released early for good behavior, he'd landed on his feet with a mop in his hand, assigned to the night shift because it was harder to fill those positions despite the better pay. Much to his surprise, he liked the repetition, solitude, and straightforward purpose. In his own way, he created order from chaos by turning dirty places clean.

For decades, he'd moved from town to town and job to job. It wasn't an easy life, but he was his own man. When he started to feel his age, he'd taken a position at a contracting company. Hustling was fine when one was young, but society started to question what went wrong in your life when you are still scrounging in your fifties. After a few years of exemplary service, they placed him in a permanent location, which suited him fine. He didn't like being sent all about town at the last minute, especially in winter.

The Detroit Institute of Arts was a daunting place, not just the majestic architecture, but all the precious items within. If anything got damaged during cleaning, it wasn't something they could simply replace and dock from his pay. From a janitorial perspective, it was a large building, and it took him two nights to get through his assigned sections before he started the rotation over again. Once he'd gotten the hang of it, he'd discovered an unforeseen perk of the job—he had a nightly private viewing of some of the finest art and exhibits in the country.

He never had to listen to someone else's commentary or

deal with someone blocking his view. He got to be alone with the pieces and in the quiet, they didn't have to contend with others' impressions and meanings. They, like Dufrane, could simply be. He was spoiled for choice when his 3:00 a.m. lunch break came, whether he was gazing at one of Diego Rivera's wall murals or dining with one of the European Old Masters. Dufrane didn't know much about art, but he knew what he liked and took the time to read the plaques and commit them to memory.

Through his time cleaning the DIA, he'd found an appreciation for history that had otherwise eluded him. When he was in school, he remembered taking history, but it was all just dates and names. Nothing really made sense or seemed to have a purpose. The DIA was different—the museum's labels also had names and dates, but they made it make sense. Everything was arranged just so, and he could see everything plain as day right in front of him—history was just a story about people trying to get by and understand what was happening to them. He could relate to that.

Dufrane had even started going to the library. Were his mother alive to witness that, she would have declared it a miracle. Books had changed since his high school history text. Sure, there were still tomes chocked full of twenty-dollar words, but there were also fully illustrated ones with explanations in plain language that gave him more information and context about the names, places, and dates he had memorized night after night. When the librarian directed him to books with various timelines of history, it blew his mind to think these people over here were doing this while those people over there were doing that—all at the same time. The more he learned, the more connections he made with the pieces in the DIA. The plaques seemed to say more than they did before, and he took pride in being part of the custodial team that helped take care of these treasures.

As Dufrane made his way down the hall, he methodically cleaned the adjacent rooms: the Kresge food court, the Ancient Middle East exhibit, and the photography room. He made the loop in good time, but picked up the pace once he approached the puppets room. Even after all this time, all those dead doll eyes gave him the willies. Dufrane always cleaned it but never dropped his guard in that section.

He breathed a sigh of relief once his cart was back in the hallway, about to embark into the Egyptian room. He unconsciously smiled as he entered his favorite nook of the museum, the place where two thousand years passed in an instant. The objects were sealed in display cases along the walls and in curios, including all the mummies. The DIA was home to numerous mummies in varying degrees of decoration and condition, but his favorite by far was Bob.

Of course, his name wasn't really Bob, but no one knew his real name. The scientists guessed that Bob had died sometime in the four hundred years before the birth of Christ, and

Dufrane felt it was a shame to be preserved like that and not have a name. So the janitor had taken to calling him Bob. He was a short guy and rather thin, but Dufrane figured that tracked—you don't get fat mummies.

The irony was not lost on Dufrane that his favorite section contained actual dead bodies while the room with lifeless marionettes spooked him. If he was being honest, Bob used to bother him too, but over time, they had come to a mutual peace once the old guy understood the janitor wasn't reckless with his mop. Dufrane took no offense—if he were as thin and dry as Bob, he wouldn't like the lug rolling around a big bucket of water, either. Stepping into the Egyptian room felt like visiting an old friend now, and there were nights when he could have sworn Bob greeted him in his own way. *Hey, how ya been? Read any good books lately?*

As Dufrane started pushing the mop, he felt a flutter in his chest. It was uncomfortable, like painful gas, and his chest tightened, making it a little difficult to breathe. He'd felt these flutters before, but they had always worked themselves out. Sometimes he wondered if he should see a doctor, but he always talked himself out of it. Simply put, Dufrane couldn't afford it. He could barely afford the pills he took for his arthritis, and those suckers were what kept him able to work.

He'd thought getting health insurance with his new permanent position was going to change things and he could start taking better care of himself. He'd learned otherwise when he tried using it—his premiums paid for the privilege of only having to pay three or four times more than he could afford instead of paying ten or twenty times more. He felt it unfair that no one went to jail for running that con, but he did three months for his hundred-buck crime. *Knowing my luck, the doctor would run a bunch of expensive tests, nothing would be wrong, and I would get stuck with the bill,* he soothed his conscience.

He chuckled at his sardonic observation when the pain intensified and shot down his left arm. He was used to hurting all over, but this was different than the arthritis. It forced him to drop his mop and take a seat on the only bench in the exhibit. He wheezed as he tried to catch his breath, but he just couldn't take in enough air. His heart raced as the pain swelled, and the last thing he remembered before passing out was thinking, *don't forget to mop under the bench.*

When he came to, he was sprawled on the floor, but the pain was gone. He thanked the good Lord and promised to go see a doctor this week. His momentary relief turned to panic when he looked at his watch and discovered he'd lost an hour. He slowly clambered to his feet—he wasn't as young as he used to be—and retrieved his mop. "Sorry, Bob," he apologized. "Gotta cut our visit short today." He bustled, took a short lunch, and managed to finish his work on time.

He was changing out of the coveralls in the janitor's closet when he realized his backup pair of glasses were no longer in the front pocket. "Shit," he cursed softly. "I don't have time for this. I'm going to miss my bus." He rewound the night to save himself from searching half of the museum in the thirty minutes before opening. His mind replayed his spell, as he had taken to calling it euphemistically.

The Egyptian room was on his way out of the building, and in his mind, it was the only place they could be. He grabbed the rest of his possessions and took the back ways, just in case anyone from the DIA was inspecting the exhibits. Dufrane went down on his hands and knees and found his glasses all the way behind the bench and he chided himself for forgetting to mop under it. As he scrambled to get back up, he heard a voice.

I have a message for you to deliver. The voice was mid-pitched, but with a timbre and rumble that only came with much deeper voices, like Barry White had just inhaled some helium. Dufrane turned his head to find the speaker, but no one was there.

"I'm sorry, I was just getting my glasses. I'll be off the floor before opening," he said apologetically. He tucked away his spares and turned to leave but was stopped in mid-step.

I have a message for you to deliver. He heard the voice again, except this time, his attention was inexplicably drawn to the wooden sarcophagus in the middle of the room. Somewhere deep inside of him, he knew his old friend was doing the talking.

"Buh…Buh…Bob?" he muttered with confusion and shock.

He did not stay long enough to get an answer. Even though he hadn't moved faster than a walk in over three decades, Isaiah Dufrane made a good show of a run. He mumbled something about missing his bus on his way out, and the security guard manning the front desk bid him goodbye.

Dufrane couldn't explain what just happened, only that it shook him to his core. He had spent most of his life working nights, and he knew the mind could play tricks on you. That moving shadow on the floor? Just a tree limb shaking in the breeze during a bright moon. That strange noise that came out of nowhere? Just the heating and cooling system kicking on and off. But try as he might, he couldn't find a reasonable explanation for hearing Bob in his head.

Despite the stares from the other bus passengers, he ran his hands over his head, feeling for lumps and sore spots to see if his head landed hard when he passed out. Never had anyone been so disappointed that they didn't have a head injury. He briefly considered going to the hospital, but with a story like his, they were likely to pink slip him or do a battery of tests on his noggin. If he couldn't afford a doctor's visit, he certainly couldn't afford an ER visit, and he knew he wasn't crazy.

When he got home, he crawled into bed as a bone-deep tiredness descended upon him. He called off sick the next day and the next, until he ran out of paid time off, hoping he could right himself, but no matter how much he slept, he couldn't seem to really wake up. He even called his doctor's office to make an appointment, but they were booked up until next week. His tiny studio apartment reeked of VapoRub, and he forced himself to slurp cans of chicken soup, even though he wasn't particularly hungry.

When he asked his company to permanently assign him somewhere else, he was brusquely denied. It was made clear that if he wanted to stay employed with the company, he'd go back to work at the Detroit Institute of Arts. He reluctantly agreed and gave himself a dose of real talk—it was a good job at a nice place, and who else was going to hire a man in his sixties? He needed to stop being a damn fool.

That's how Dufrane found himself a week later, suited up and rolling down the promenade once again, mop in hand. Whoever they had fill in for him did serviceable work, but he could tell they took shortcuts based on how hard he had to clean the neglected nooks and crannies. An hour into his shift, he started to feel a bit more like his old self with each pass of the mop. He still felt wrung out, but each moment seemed to wash a little more of the exhaustion from him. He even enjoyed his lunch break with Bouguereau's *The Nut Gatherers*. He always wondered what mischievous thing the fair-haired girl had said to make the raven-haired one ponder so.

Dufrane worked his way through all the other first-floor exhibits before he found himself outside the Egyptian room. From the doorway, it felt cold, heavy, unwelcoming, and perhaps even a little angry. For the first time in five years, he'd honestly rather be in the puppets room. But he'd already cleaned that room, and Bob was waiting for him.

"Heya Bob? How're, uh, things today, old man?" he tentatively asked while crossing the threshold. The lack of response calmed him down and soon he was back into his meditative state. Swish, swish, swish, wring, dunk, wring, swish, swish, swish. He'd worked his way back to the entrance when he heard the voice again.

I have a message for you to deliver.

This time, he didn't run. He couldn't run. "Where do you need me to go?" The words fell out of his mouth mindlessly.

You must go to the place called Zug Island.

Dufrane felt his head nod and the mop dropped out of his hands. "I will do as you command."

Bob relayed his message, and Dufrane felt the words burn into him like the chapters and verses of the Bible that he'd been forced to memorized as a child. They were words he would never forget. Without a second thought, Isaiah Dufrane walked out of the Detroit Institute of Arts into the cold night, steadily making his way south to Zug Island.

*****

George Barnes arrived at work long before the sun came up, relieving the overnight guard who manned the gate into Zug Island. Some might find the early start a negative, but he didn't mind. Working off hours meant missing rush hour traffic both ways, and he got paid to watch the gorgeous sunrises over Windsor. In summer, the sun rose early enough that he could enjoy it with a thermos of coffee at hand and his still-hot breakfast steaming out of the insulated bag he always brought with him. His wife believed in three hot square meals a day, even if he could only share one with his family on work days.

It was still dark this morning as he stowed his personal possessions and checked all the systems. They were always functioning per spec, but he confirmed it at the beginning of his shift nonetheless because that's what he was supposed to do, and he knew better than to tempt misfortune—the day he didn't check would be the day they malfunctioned. If his brief stint in the Navy had taught him anything, it was do what you're supposed to *every time* and if something bad happens, it ain't your fault.

Once he finished his rounds, he cracked open his thermos and got to the second major perk of his job: he had a lot of down time to himself. Barnes loved his growing family, but he also appreciated the quiet of his little guard station. Things at home had become exponentially chaotic with the arrival of the twins, not that he would trade them for anything in the world. It was just nice to get paid while having a place to be alone with his thoughts and read a book—a sheer luxury when there are young children in the house.

He sipped his first cup of coffee, turned on his inexpensive tablet, and picked up where he'd left off, hoping to finish the book before the first arrivals came. His busiest time was the morning and afternoon shift change, during which he checked IDs coming in and out. There were only two businesses on the island—Detroit Iron Works and Discretion Minerals—and with only one entrance onto Zug Island, it was pretty easy to guard the choke point of a non-commercial gate. Truth be told, he wasn't sure why the gate required a guard around the clock, especially with all the high-tech security systems they had in place, but he never voiced his opinions as long as someone was willing to sign his paycheck. All in all, he'd had worse gigs, and Georgie never was one to look a gift horse in the mouth.

He chuffed as the good guys prevailed in the twenty-eighth title of the men's adventure series he'd read as a kid. Back then, they were spines lined up on his dad's shelf, but now they were little icons just a finger tap away. He was about to click "buy next in series" when he saw a figure walking over the bridge leading to the island. He'd worked here for almost ten years, and he had never encountered a pedestrian employee before. Industrial workers and executives were hardly the walk-to-work type. The island itself was tucked against the river and surrounded by industrial and commercial properties. Sure, there were some houses to the northwest, but the area was rife with that unique Detroit blight—lone houses surrounded by fields that were once neighborhoods.

Barnes put away his tablet and got a better look at the figure. He was an older black man dressed in blue work coveralls but no coat. His gait was stilted and jerky, which shifted Barnes's mind away from wondering if he'd have to call the police to what he should do if the old timer was in trouble or perhaps having some mental problems. He knew confused elderly people might walk out of their house and not know where they were going or how to get back; right-thinking people don't go outside without a jacket this late in October.

Barnes stepped out of the hut and stood officiously behind the bar of the gate. "Sir, this is private property. I'm going to have to ask you to leave," he yelled. It came out a little more gruff than he intended. "Is there someone I can call to come get you?" he added less brusquely. There would be cars soon, and it wouldn't be safe for the old man to be walking on the bridge.

Without acknowledging the guard's call, Isaiah Dufrane persisted in his advance. Barnes wondered if maybe he was hard of hearing, and waited until he was closer to repeat himself. "Sir, you can't enter. This is private property. Is there anyone I can call to come get you?"

Dufrane lurched forward and opened his mouth. He spoke slowly but deliberately, "I seek the Faithful One on behalf of the true keeper of the dead. There has been a theft in the Valley of the Magi. Hor-Nebwy requests the servant named the Hobgoblin. He must come to us. We call in our debt." After he spoke, Dufrane waited motionless outside the gate.

He felt neither the cold of the night nor the wind coming off the river. The achy exhaustion of walking the seven miles from the DIA to Zug Island did not register. He had a mission, and he wouldn't be done until he had delivered the message to the Faithful One herself.

Something stirred inside Barnes upon hearing the old man's words, and he stepped inside the guard station. He reached across his console to the top corner and pressed a red button he had never seen before now. Were he thinking clearly, he would have wondered where it had come from, but it felt like he was acting on instinct. A precisely enunciated tenor came out of the speaker next to the button. "This is LaSalle."

"This is George Barnes at the guard station," he stated clearly. "We have a special visitor."

Chapter Six

Nalin Oliver Buchholz lazily roused on his high-thread-count Egyptian cotton sheets. They were so soft and silky against his bare skin, it was like sleeping in moving water. He opened his dark brown eyes to a foot lying next to his face. It was a lovely foot—a smooth tanned size seven with a graceful arch and five slim, impeccably pedicured toes—but that didn't excuse its current location. He cradled the ankle gently in his hand with the intent of moving it to a more suitable place, but the contact woke his guest.

The lanky brunette groggily moaned as she stretched all five-foot-ten of herself, and his eyes traced the cut of her lean quads and calves of the leg in his hand. Delicious memories of last night returned and he smiled. *That's right, she's an Olympic swimmer.*

"Morning," his companion said groggily from the foot of the bed, propping herself up on the pillow she'd used through the night. "Do you always wake up women by grabbing their ankles?"

"You seemed into it last night," he joked before planting

a light kiss on the instep. She giggled but didn't pull away, so he started working his way up the smooth muscular leg. He was just past the knee when his phone rang out, blaring the arpeggioed first rift of Johnny Rivers's version of "Secret Agent Man."

Much to both their dismay, he stopped his advance. "Sorry, gotta answer," he apologized, fishing out the phone from under something small and silky.

"I'm here," he answered, rolling nude from under the covers and walking to the kitchen for a little privacy. He smiled as he felt his partner's eyes following every step. She'd admitted that she had a thing for tall, dark, and handsome, and at 6'3" and 185 pounds of lean muscle wrapped in a light mocha skin, he knew it was hard to find someone who better fit the bill than him.

David LaSalle's distinct voice, as cool as the kitchen tiles beneath Buchholz's feet, came over the line. "We need you to finish the job faster than expected." Buchholz's brow furrowed at the order; he'd only been on the mission for a few days and the briefing had suggested a window of several weeks.

"How quickly?" he asked, pulling supplies for coffee out of the cabinets.

"As soon as possible," LaSalle replied. "Your next mission is already lined up once you're done."

"Understood," Buchholz responded blithely as to not alert his guest to the seriousness of the call. He packed the grounds for the espresso machine. "Anything else?"

"Leader is indifferent to your solution method."

A grin spread across Buchholz's face. "Excellent."

LaSalle didn't like the tone of his reply. "But if discretion is possible—"

"Of course," he reassured LaSalle. "I'll let you know when I'm ready to fly out."

"I'll ready for your arrival," LaSalle confirmed before hanging up.

Buchholz removed the phone from his ear and started the brew. The dark liquid dripped from twin spouts into the Bodum Pavina double-walled demitasses. The seaside condo filled with the smell of it. He worked the milk into a light froth and wiped down the spigot after he was done. He returned with two perfect cappuccinos.

"You have to get going?" she said as she sat up and pulled the sheets with her. Buchholz made no such attempt at modesty.

"Work calls," he lamented as he handed her a cup. "But I would never turn you out without coffee. I'm not a complete barbarian."

She smirked at his brand of humor and savored her first sip. "So, what is it you do again?" she probed.

He raised an eyebrow and said playfully, "I could tell you, but then I'd have to kill you."

"Ugh, that's a terrible line," she groaned, but he noticed that she laughed at it nonetheless. It was throaty and sincere, and he regretted not being able to finish what he'd started.

She started circling the rim of her cup with her thumbs and looked up at him coquettishly, playing along with his ridiculous story. "So, do secret agents need to take a shower before heading out?"

His body involuntarily answered for him, and she set down her cup. With a flip of the wrist, she turned down the sheet and rose from the bed. The curve of her hip and swell of her small, pert breasts was breathtaking. She sashayed to the bathroom, and a few seconds after she disappeared, he heard the shower softly turn on. Nalin Buchholz—codename Hobgoblin—quickly finished his coffee and joined her. He knew when duty called.

*****

The harsh Florida sun beat down on Brickell Avenue, and the gleaming buildings that lined the street labored to offset the rising temperature. The unseasonal heat wave persisted, driving the thermometer over ninety degrees before the clock had even reached noon. The AC in the dandelion-yellow Lotus Evora carrying Buchholz was on full blast until it drove into the shade of the parking garage beneath Grupo Financiero Banorte USA's new headquarters.

He backed into a parking space and checked his visor mirror to make sure his disguise was working. From his initial reconnaissance, he knew he would be on camera the entire time. He exited his vehicle carrying two matching leather suitcases and pressed the button for the elevator, counting no less than three cameras using his peripheral vision.

On the elevator ride to the twenty-second floor, Buchholz put down the cases to adjust his suit and tie his two-inch platform shoes, deftly concealed by the slightly long cut of his pants. He also ran a hand through his hair to ensure the cameras behind the mirrors got a good look at his clear pale skin, blond hair, and blue eyes. He wanted to make sure that anyone reviewing the security footage after the fact would follow the trail of breadcrumbs to a dead end. Once he was satisfied with the ruse, he retrieved the cases and he focused his will—*was mich nicht umbringt, macht mich stärker.*

A bell chimed once the elevator reached his floor, and the doors opened into a large lobby. The furnishings were fresh and stylish, much like the receptionist sitting at her heritage desk in front of the only door that led deeper into the office. She was pretty and dressed to the nines, with flawless hair and nails. She wore way more makeup than she needed, but it was applied tastefully.

Buchholz stepped forward and smiled. "I'm here to see Mr. Morimoto, please," he said once he reached the desk.

"Who may I say is here?" she asked politely, pulling up her scheduling software on her computer. She didn't remember seeing any appointments on Mr. Morimoto's calendar when she arrived this morning.

Buchholz unfurled his will and wrapped it around the pretty woman's head like a spider web. "The person telling you it's time to take an hour-long lunch," he answered with a grin. He shrugged gallantly. "Treat yourself."

The reception stared into his flirtatious blue eyes and returned the smile. "I'm sorry, I can't help you," she replied as she opened the bottom drawer and extracted her purse. "It's my lunch break." Dumbly, she rose from her chair and summoned the elevator down.

He waited in the lobby until the lights above the elevator were blinking toward the ground floor. Then, he slipped through the door and strode down a hallway lined with inoffensive art. It was a short walk to the southeastern corner office, and he politely knocked on the solid oak door.

Morimoto was startled by the rap. He wasn't expecting anyone, and the receptionist would have called him if he had an unscheduled visitor that passed her scrutiny. He put aside his work and assumed a commanding tone. "Come in."

"Hello, Mr. Morimoto," Buchholz said as he entered the oversized office, closing the door behind him. He knew there would be no cameras in here—it wouldn't do to spy on the executives. Mr. Morimoto was sitting at a mahogany desk that formed the hypotenuse to the corner of the glass-walled office. To the left was another door leading to an exterior patio upon which a couch and chairs looked out toward the ocean.

Morimoto was a young man, no more than thirty, with perfectly manicured nails. Buchholz judged him to be a power-seeker by the affected demeanor he was donning. He had the air of one who served but wanted to be on top. "Forgive the unannounced visit. As you know, my employer likes to work off the books whenever possible." Buchholz bowed slightly to put him at ease. "I was told to give you this." He held out one of the suitcases.

Morimoto did not stand nor accept the proffered case, but instead inquired, "Told by whom?"

"I think you know, Mr. Morimoto," Buchholz intoned knowingly. The three-act play of emotions played at high speed in Morimoto's mind. His first instinct was fear at the oblique reference to the La Nueva Plaza drug cartel for whom he had laundered millions. Then, his greed kicked in—he had already held back his cut of the clean money, so any additional payout was truly beyond the pale. Last, the anxiety set in. Was this some sort of test? Or maybe a trick? Was he supposed to refuse the money?

Buchholz could see the wheels spinning and ingratiated himself further. "Consider it a gift for services rendered. He's very appreciative of the work you've done and looks forward to future endeavors. In fact, he's grateful to all the employees of Grupo Financiero Banorte USA and asks that you distribute his thanks as you see fit."

Morimoto almost smiled—he was suspicious of unforeseen

gifts, but he understood bribery. The cartel wanted him to use some of this money to bring in more like-minded associates, and he was being compensated for his connections. He kept his face neutral and waved for Buchholz to approach, patting the center of his desk. Buchholz laid the suitcase down, carefully positioning the locks to face Morimoto. Had the businessman been more suspicious, he might have noticed how gently the courier had set it down, but his mind was already counting the stacks within. "The lock's code is 666," Buchholz informed him and backed up to give a modicum of privacy to examine the contents.

Morimoto paused, but only briefly before letting out a curt laugh at the twisted humor. In his culture, talk of demons was taboo and invited bad luck, but he understood the cartel had a strong affection for the transgressive—to name it strips it of its power, and who was tough enough to take on La Nueva Plaza? He spun the gold-plated disks until they showed all 6s and opened the briefcase. Absolute silence filled the air as a misty blackness leapt out of it, knocking Morimoto out of his chair and onto his back.

From Buchholz's position, he could see the signs of a deadly struggle, but he couldn't hear a thing, not even his own breathing. He pulled out his gun and waited for it to be over. The tussle abruptly came to an end, and when the tip of the shadow popped over the desk, it was met with an unnaturally silent banishing bullet fired from the barrel of Buchholz's

Walther CCP. The blackness and the bullet vanished, and sound returned to the room. Once he confirmed that Morimoto was dead, Buchholz opened the other suitcase, set the timer, and left it underneath the desk.

Buchholz was back in his Lotus driving north when the bomb finally went off, taking out the entire corner of the twenty-second floor. He took glee at the rising smoke in the passenger side mirror. He was sure he'd catch some flack when he returned to the Salt Mine, but he didn't believe for one second that Leader didn't know what to expect when he had free rein to wrap things up quickly. There was a reason she had given him Hobgoblin as a codename—any problem could be solved with explosives, and knowing just how much constituted the right amount was his specialty.

He was well out of the neighborhood when the first of the emergency vehicles passed him on their way toward the explosion. He knew their protocols inside and out, and by the time they assessed the scene, determined that there weren't any other risks, and started looking at security footage, he would be on his way to Detroit. But first, he had to make another stop for specialty supplies.

Wynwood was one of the roughest areas of Miami, but Hobgoblin always made a pilgrimage there at least twice a year, specifically to the Circle of Life Funeral Home. It was a modest family business run by two pillars of the community, the Washington brothers. When a family couldn't afford funerary services for a loved one, Circle of Life would take care of it, free of charge.

When he entered the building, there was a service going on—the chapel doors were closed and he heard the indistinct echo of amplified voices. He plopped down on a bench in the central room and fired up his phone to play through a level of his most-recent game obsession. When the organ finally started and the doors opened, he put his phone away and respectfully tilted his head down as the flow of mourners headed to the parking lot. Once it was down to a few stragglers, he entered the sanctuary, looking for the guy who ran the place.

Larry Washington was speaking with the family, but tactfully nudged his head in the direction of the center of the funeral home once he saw Hobgoblin step through the double doors. Buchholz made his way into the private inner waiting room, knowing he wouldn't have to wait long—a visit from Hobgoblin paid Larry way more than any funeral.

Washington dropped his solemn mask as soon as he burst through the doors. "How the hell are ya, Bill?" he greeted Hobgoblin with a firm, friendly handshake and pat on the shoulder. "I hadn't expected to see you for several more months."

"I'm great, Larry," he replied, "I've just had an unexpected vacation; my great aunt died."

"I'm sorry for your loss," Washington said reflexively while his face instantly rearranged itself into one of empathy.

"I'm not," he quipped. "She left me ten thousand dollars…"

The exacting figure and the drop off in his voice spoke volumes to Washington.

"And you want to make a pre-payment?" the mortician spoke in code.

"Precisely."

Washington clapped his hands together. "Sounds great. Step inside and see what we can do for you." He led Hobgoblin down to the basement where the real work happened. The Circle of Life Funeral Home worked closely with the Miami-Dade medical examiner, often functioning as a waystation for unclaimed bodies when they'd piled up in the county facilities. On the rare cases when someone claimed a body, they got that business, although it was general practice at Circle of Life to hand out free funerals for those who really couldn't pay.

More often than not, the dead went unclaimed, and Circle of Life was contracted to process them, which was where the Washington brothers made most of their profits—selling human remains on the magical market. As long as the county got a labeled box of ashes, it didn't much care if something was missing or if one body got stretched to fill more than one box. That was why they handed out funerals for free—it generated an astounding amount of good karma and there were always people who couldn't pay.

Once they were out of earshot, Washington got down to business, "So what do you need today, Bill? More bodies?"

"Yep. Just the usual today," Hobgoblin replied matter-offactly.

"And how many?" the mortician asked nonchalantly.

"I think I can pick up six this time," he answered. "Price still the same?"

"Correct," Washington affirmed, nodding a little too much at the money that was about to come his way. He'd done enough business with Hobgoblin to know it would be in cash wrapped in standard stacks, a hundred bills at a time. They entered the rectangular storage room, which was nearly the length of the funeral home. Both of the long walls were lined with three-stack cadaver refrigerator freezers with a total storage space of more than two hundred bodies. "I'm a bit low—only got twenty bodies available right now, but you should still be able to find something of interest."

Washington opened the first of many cubicles, showcasing each corpse and stating the ethnicity, sex, estimated age, cause of death, missing limbs and organs, and any other unusual health conditions. For the incomplete bodies, he listed the discount off the standard price—when someone pays ten thousand dollars for a corpse, they expect all the parts and pieces, and the Washington brothers prided themselves on running an honest business that was above board, even if it was technically illegal. Practitioners of the arts were not the sort you wanted to cheat.

It took twenty minutes for Hobgoblin to pick six, and Washington quickly loaded the cash in the counting machine for verification. Once the deal was sealed, Buchholz pulled the titanium chain from around his neck and opened the fish amulet that dangled at the end. One by one, each of the corpses was sucked inside. Washington never asked about the enchanted trinket nor what Buchholz—or Bill, as he knew him—did with the bodies. Part of the sticker price was for discretion and minding his own damn business.

Honestly, Buchholz didn't know exactly *how* the amulet worked, just that when he needed to plant a body, he'd simply open the amulet and think about what he needed. Then, presto, the closest thing he had stashed within would pop back out. The amulet could even mold the retrieved body to match a particular individual if he wanted—down to the dental and DNA.

It was a useful piece of kit for his line of work, but it wasn't without hiccups. Occasionally the bodies he'd put in would go missing or come out with a bite taken out of them. One time, a corpse had come out undead and quite pissed about it. The amulet had puzzled even Chloe and Dot—the conjoined twins who ran the Mine's research and records department. They had traced it back to the third century CE and thought it of ancient Christian origin, mostly likely of fossor make. The fossors were catacomb gravediggers in Rome responsible for Christians who died of obvious illnesses, such as plague. Having a necklace to transport such bodies or simply make them disappear made sense to him.

He tucked his amulet back under his shirt and made his

farewells. As long as people died anonymously in Miami, Buchholz would patronize the Circle of Life—it was as close as one could get to renewable, ethically sourced corpses.

Chapter Seven

Detroit, Michigan, USA
21st of October, 6:42 p.m. (GMT-4)

"Hobgoblin to see you, ma'am," LaSalle announced as he opened the door to Leader's office. Buchholz strode into the office and a sharp scent of antiseptic hit his nostrils. Neither Leader nor the wall of muscle that was her secretary-slash-bodyguard seemed bothered by it, so he simply took one of the unusually wide seats in front of her desk.

"Thank you, David. That will be all for now," Leader replied from behind her desk as she switched gears and paperwork for the agent in front of her. LaSalle exited the room and closed the door behind him. She did not deign to stand or address Hobgoblin's entrance; it had been a trying day with more unknowns than at its start.

Buchholz silently waited while she organized a stack of folders on her desk and then placed them in the filing cabinet behind her. Even when not focused on him, he could feel her intimidating presence. The desk partially concealed her diminutive stature, but it hardly mattered that he was over a foot taller than her and in his prime. Buchholz always felt small in front of Leader, and the oversized seating didn't help.

The first time he had entered this office was during his final interview. At the time, he was *Kommando Spezialkräfte* operating in the West Asian Theater, and he had seen things he couldn't forget, but unlike all the other horrors he had witnessed fighting wars and insurgency, he simply couldn't understand what he had seen. When he went looking for answers, Leader was on the other end, and that's how Buchholz became Hobgoblin. It wasn't until he met Chloe and Dot that he understood the chairs were wider than normal to make the librarians comfortable and all the chairs were the same size so they could sit in any of the chairs, not just *their* chair.

Of course, that didn't discount their use in psychological gamesmanship. Leader was never one to waste an opportunity, and if the unintended side effect of making the twins feel welcomed was making everyone else feel small, so be it. Buchholz never put anything past Leader—two birds, one stone, and plausible deniability was her jam.

When she swiveled around, she was holding a green folder labeled AGENT RESTRICTED – SM EYES ONLY. She turned her hawkish gray eyes on him. "Early this morning, we were contacted by Hor-Nebwy requesting our assistance in a private matter. What connection do you have with Hor-Nebwy?"

Buchholz felt the weight of her stare. Now that her full attention was on him, his chest involuntarily tightened and he had to concentrate to breathe normally. It was always that way with her. He scoured his brain but came up short—no Hor-Nebwys. "I've never heard of him," he answered truthfully.

The pressure let up marginally as she pondered his reply but redoubled with her next question. "Then why has he requested you personally?"

He shook his head side-to-side. "I have no idea. Which of my aliases did he use?"

"None. He asked for the Hobgoblin," she replied, uncharacteristically peeved. *Then again, he always did call things by their true nature*, she thought as an aside. Leader opened the folder and turned it to face Buchholz. "Since you're unfamiliar with Hor-Nebwy and the Valley of the Magi, I'll quickly bring you up to speed with his abridged history. Full information is in the file." The intensity of her will lessened, and he felt it a little easier to breathe.

"Hor-Nebwy lived sometime in the twenty-second century BCE. He was one of the earliest pharaohs and a strong practitioner of magic. He died in battle and his body was left in the sands, where it naturally mummified. He rose several years later and played a key role in the death-obsessed nature of the Ancient Egyptians for several centuries. He retreated from the mortal realm and sequestered himself in a magically protected locale called the Valley of the Magi, where he creates tombs for magicians who want to enter the Egyptian afterlife."

"Like the Valley of the Kings?" Buchholz inquired. He had never heard of Hor-Nebwy or the Valley of the Magi, and his pride was a little bruised. Even though he was a relative newcomer to the esoteric, he liked to think he was in the know.

Leader winced at the comparison—that was exactly the sort of thing not to say in front of Hor-Nebwy. *Why did he have to ask for my demolitions specialist?* "Sort of, but not really. That's like comparing the Magh Meall to Yellowstone, and Hor-Nebwy will not be as gracious as I am about the unfavorable association," she warned.

Buchholz nodded curtly—anything that spooked Leader was worth being wary of. "Okay. So what's this mummy want with me?"

"Something has been stolen from the Valley of the Magi, and he wants you to retrieve it," she answered solemnly.

"So I'm looking for a graverobber?" he puzzled.

"Not just any graverobber. Someone or something who knows about the Valley of the Magi and was able to circumvent its considerable magical security."

Buchholz shifted uncomfortably in his seat. He could understand if Hor-Nebwy wanted something blown up or disappeared, but he was hardly the best at security or retrieval. *If only Wilson were still here*, he groused. Despite his reservations, he knew not going wasn't a choice. "What was stolen?"

"No idea," she responded with a corresponding shrug. "Hor-Nebwy is very private and has chosen to give you the details in person." The implication sent goose bumps up his arm. *What kind of being can convince Leader to accept such secrecy in a request?*

A flashing light started blinking on her desk, and Leader pressed a button. "Yes?"

LaSalle's voice came over the speaker. "I've booked Hobgoblin on a red-eye to Luxor. It departs at 9:05 p.m. His mission package, instructions, and detailed briefing are already in his office." Both of them looked at their watches.

"Thank you, David." She released the button and addressed Hobgoblin once more, "I shouldn't need to say this, but I will for clarity. This is a diplomatic, fact-finding mission, not your usual elimination. Hor-Nebwy should be extended courtesies above and beyond what may seem reasonable. As long as you follow the etiquette we've provided, you should be fine. Pay close attention to everything, Hobgoblin. This may be the only time you have to gather clues about the theft, and we want Hor-Nebwy on our side. *And* we want more information about him and the Valley of the Magi for our files. Keep your eyes open."

"You can count on me, Leader," he said resolutely. He closed the file on the desk and tucked it under his arm. She nodded to him, her way of dismissing him and wishing him luck. She had already moved on to the next file when he opened the door. The momentary easing of her directed will was too much for him to pass up, and he playfully asked, "You want me to bring you back a souvenir from the pyramids?"

Leader didn't look up from her desk. "You have a plane to

catch, Hobgoblin."

He gave a crisp "Yes, ma'am" and bowed before closing the door behind him. In the solitude of her office, Leader put down her pen and pinched the bridge of her nose between her eyes. *It had to be Hobgoblin...*

Buchholz pressed his left eye and right hand to the scanner once inside the elevator. The metal box shuddered as it started its brief descent one floor. He wound his way down the saline passage to the row of agent offices until he found his name on the door. All agents of the Salt Mine had an office on the fifth floor—there were always reports to be filed and dailies to be read. That said, some were more used that others, and Buchholz was definitely more of a field man. His definition of hell on earth was rotting away behind some desk.

The scanner recognized his palm, and the neglected office came into view when he flipped on the light switch. Everything was pretty much the same as the day he had been assigned to the office, except for the computer and high-efficiency lightbulbs in the sockets. Buchholz didn't see the point of customizing and decorating a space within which he intended to spend as little time as possible. He put his mission briefing on his dusty mid-century metal desk and pried open the nondescript box sitting at its center.

Buchholz was used to receiving mission-specific equipment because every mission was unique in its own way. Even the most straightforward jobs required specific banishing bullets.

He was a little crestfallen when a visit to the sixth floor wasn't mentioned at his briefing. Not seeing Harold Weber—the Salt Mine's inventor and quartermaster extraordinaire—meant he wasn't going to be getting any fun toys for this trip. Still, he was curious to see what was deemed essential kit when meeting with a mummy. He had worked with strange and mysterious before, but not this particular breed.

He put the paperwork to one side and dug deeper into the box only to find a pair of woven reed shoes with ridiculous-looking recurved points atop a single piece of linen cloth. Buchholz picked up the nestled booklet and flipped through—apparently, the cloth was called a shendyt, the preferred clothing of ancient Egypt. Thankfully, there were also instructions on how to fold it into something like a kilt along with a matching quick-guide to pharaonic etiquette.

On the bottom of the box was a small personal hygiene case filled with various scented oils. Buchholz opened a few and gave them a cursory whiff test before skimming the detailed instructions on how to bathe and anoint himself before he walked out into the Egyptian desert at night dressed as what he felt was a caricature of an ancient Egyptian.

"Well, that's not going to attract attention at all," he derisively said aloud as he carefully repacked the box. He'd have hours in the air to get caught up, but precious time to get packed and to the airport.

*****

"Sir, would you like something to drink," the stewardess asked Buchholz as she pushed her cart down the aisle.

He looked up from his reading and found a friendly face smiling at him. Were the mission different, he would order a cocktail and spend the long flight with her, but he had a lot of work to do. "Just black coffee, thanks," he answered politely without a hint of flirtation.

She poured him a steaming cup from the carafe nestled on the top. "We'll be turning down the cabin lights in an hour for passengers to sleep," she informed him as she handed him his beverage with a napkin. Their hands touched, and she added, "Let me know if you need anything during your flight."

He knew that tone and bemoaned his fate. She was just his type—pretty, a stewardess, and into him. "Thanks, I'm good with just the coffee for now."

Buchholz faithfully returned to the Salt Mine's history of Hor-Nebwy and the Valley of the Magi. He knew he had a reputation as the fast and loose agent, and that didn't bother him one bit. Despite his cavalier "shoot first, ask questions later" style, he always took his responsibilities seriously. He got the job done and he never left a fellow agent in the lurch— that's what counted in his book. It didn't help that he was quick-witted and the first to crack a joke to lighten the mood. Their line of work was somber enough.

What was often mistaken for inattentiveness during group meetings was a byproduct of being an extremely fast reader with very good recall. He wasn't anywhere close to what Chloe and Dot could do with their eidetic memories, but his rate of retention broke the curve in more than one study when the *Kommando Spezialkräfte* tested him.

He started with the pictures, or illustrations as they were in this case. The first displayed Hor-Nebwy as the traditional movie mummy, emaciated and fully wrapped in linen except for the eyes and mouth, and bedecked with gold jewelry. The second was him unwrapped, wearing only a shendyt and the same jewelry. Buchholz examined the taut desiccated skin drawn over the skeletal body—it reminded him of the photos of Holocaust survivors he was shown as a boy, so his people would never forget what they had done in their collective madness.

The artist had captured a definite intensity in the stare and his commanding stance in both illustrations, although Buchholz did not detect blatant aggression in either. Hor-Nebwy was one used to being obeyed because it was his divine right. Buchholz memorized the face as he always did, although he was at a loss at how he was supposed to pick Hor-Nebwy out of a crowd of mummies. *Are there going to be a bunch of mummies wandering the Valley of the Magi?* he wondered for the first time.

He brought himself back to task by refreshing himself on

mummies and seeing if any new information had been added to canon. By definition, mummies were preserved dead bodies animated by the reflection of the soul that once dwelled within the body. It wasn't the actual soul of the living creature that once inhabited the physical body, but a near perfect match, meaning they had the same basic personalities and quirks, but were immune to all normal soul-affecting magics since they weren't technically alive. Ergo, mummies couldn't be charmed, drained, dominated, or confused. There was a time when the Mine used the term "anti-soul" to describe the animating force of mummies, but it fell out of favor once it was definitively confirmed that mummies had no intrinsic tendencies toward evil, unlike most other undead. As a general rule, Chloe and Dot strove for precise terminology.

He scrolled down the list of strengths and weaknesses, and didn't see anything new. Mummies were very durable, in part due to the fact that their skin was as tough as cuir bouilli—boiled leather—but also because they didn't feel pain. A mummy could take a licking and keep on ticking. Despite their gauntness, they were as strong as the strongest humans, and they could regrow lost limbs, including heads if given enough time. But their scariest asset was their magic: all mummies were well-versed in practicing the arcane arts. Some were even masters, which was to be expected given their state of conditional immortality.

Many of the conventional measures against supernatural

creatures didn't work on mummies. Salt and holy symbols were worthless, cold iron didn't matter, and banishment bullets didn't affect them beyond the damage from a fired ballistic. Basically, the only thing that mummies did not like was fire and water. It seemed pretty obvious why a desiccated husk of a body wrapped in linen would be vulnerable to fire, but water was just as bad. Excess levels of humidity undermined the toughness of their skin, and if submerged, a mummy could melt away. Their aversion to water made fire that much more dangerous to them. The file ended with a list of known mummies along with their last-known location. There weren't many names and Buchholz noted the particular absence of Hor-Nebwy from the list.

Buchholz closed that file and stretched his legs in the galley before diving into the Valley of the Magi file. The first thing he pulled up was the hand-drawn map dated February 12th, 1936 that roughly laid out the valley. Its design was similar to the Valley of Kings outside of Luxor. The only apparent difference was that Hor-Nebwy's realm was larger, with more branches than its mundane version.

Now that he knew what the area looked like, he flipped back to the text and started from the beginning. As he read, a sense of dread came over Hobgoblin. Hor-Nebwy didn't just reside in the Valley of the Magi; he created it. He wasn't on the mummy list because creating his own parallel pocket dimension made him a power who happened to also be a mummy.

"Shit," Buchholz cursed. Now he understood why Leader was so insistent on doing things a certain way in the briefing. *Power* was the generic term for incredibly powerful beings, creatures such as gods, demi-gods, avatars, and other various and unique elder creatures. They were beyond dangerous, even the well-meaning ones. He knew the Salt Mine kept a list of powers, but its security clearance was above his pay grade. None of the agents had access unless Leader deemed them "need to know." Buchholz had never encountered a power before, but he knew one thing—when he walked into the desert in Egypt, he'd end up in the Valley of the Magi, completely at the mercy of an ancient mummified power. Knowing he'd been asked for by name didn't make him feel any better.

As per form, the profile ended with an enumeration of all known dangers and a catalogue of all the creatures that were magically prevented from entering. The Valley of the Magi was warded against everything imaginable. Hobgoblin had broken in to a lot of places, mundane and magical, and he had never seen such security. The sheer amount of energy to maintain so many wards was staggering. Try as he might, he could not think of a magic-using creature that wasn't included. Even some *individual* creatures were warded against—by *name*. All the names were redacted entries, which could only mean they were other powers that Leader didn't feel he needed to know about.

Fulcrum would have loved this guy, he thought morosely

as he looked out the window to the light-speckled land thirty thousand feet below. *Probably had posters of him on his wall when he was a kid.*

Reality sunk in—whoever or whatever broke into the Valley of the Magi outwitted the heavily guarded fortress of an ancient power and he, out of all the Salt Mine agents available, was supposed to track them down. He closed the file and pressed the button to summon the stewardess while he stewed in his predicament. He decided to reread the instructions LaSalle had given him on etiquette, cleaning, and anointment, how to fold that stupid skirt, and performing the ritual. But first, he needed a stiff drink.

The pretty stewardess came up the aisle and switched off his call light. "How can I help you, sir?" she asked in a honeyed voice.

"I need a glass of your oldest Scotch, neat," he replied firmly.

Chapter Eight

Buchholz felt like a fool. The red-and-white-striped shendyt was bad enough by itself, but the pointy-toed shoes pushed the outfit into the ridiculous. He also smelled like a perfumery had exploded on him. He could live with the ludicrous getup, but it pained him to leave his hotel without any weapons. The briefing was very clear on that—walk into the desert at night with nothing but the stupid shoes and farcical kilt. He'd always carried a weapon of some kind when he worked, but then again, he had never been sent on a diplomatic fact-finding mission with a power.

He mentally reviewed the incantations of the ritual in the back seat of the hired car while the driver kept sneaking glances in his rearview mirror. It wasn't every day he had a foreigner dressed in costume muttering to himself in the back of his car, but his money spent like any other fare. The evening bustle of Luxor passed by his window, and they drove in silence through the crowded, dusty streets until the car stopped at a ferry terminal. The driver rolled down his window and started a heated conversation with the attendant.

Buchholz knew Modern Standard Arabic, but that was the language of newspapers, books, television, and official documents. Spoken colloquial Arabic had many different dialects, and they were not all mutually intelligible to each other. Because of his location, he guessed the driver was speaking Masri, aka Egyptian Arabic, but he had never served in Africa and only picked up a few words in the rapid exchange—something about "crazy" and "money."

Officially, ferry service between the east and west bank ran twenty-four hours a day, but in practice, local traffic was well past its peak and twenty-four hours a day became a flexible idea. There were always smaller boats that would take passengers across, but Buchholz wanted a ferry so his current driver could take him all the way to the Valley of the Kings. The fewer transactions he had to perform in this outfit, the better, as that meant fewer people to remember him.

"A problem?" Buchholz asked in English when the attendant walked away mid-sentence. He had no problem playing the dumb foreigner—people tended to speak more freely when they thought you couldn't understand what they were saying, even if in this case he wasn't picking up more than a word here and there.

"No problem, no problem!" the driver enthusiastically assured his passenger in a thick accent.

Buchholz sat back and nodded. He couldn't count the number of countries he'd been in where "No problem!"

eventually worked itself out given enough shouting and time, especially if bills exchanged hands. "Okay, but I am in a hurry, so please make it quick."

"No problem, no problem!" the driver repeated. "You an actor?"

The shadow across the back seat hid his slight grin. "Something like that," Buchholz remarked. He did feel like someone running lines before a big audition.

That appeared to satisfy the driver's curiosity. Armed with that information, he got out of the car and walked to the attendant's station. After a vigorous exchange, the two men reached a consensus and money was exchanged. The driver returned to his car and the attendant to a small ferry docked to one side. It was a bit of a production, but after a few minutes, the small vessel's motor fired up, and it taxied into place and dropped a ramp. Between the overhead lights and his headlights, the driver carefully eased the car onto the vessel.

Soon, they were chugging along, and the dark waters stretched out in front of Buchholz—the Nile, one of humanity's mother rivers. It was his first time to see it in person, and he took a mental picture, adding it to the others he'd visited: the Indus, the Ganges, the Yellow, the Yangzi. He'd also seen the Tigris, but he never willingly revisited those memories.

As with so many other landmarks of note, the thing itself was unimpressive—at best, an everyday miracle like sunrise or a rainbow. What held his interest was the concept of the thing;

that vastly overshadowed the physical reality of the place. This river had allowed humanity to form one of its first civilizations. In the days before the Aswan Dam, the Nile would have been at its zenith, replenishing the banks with silt and ensuring the coming harvest. Now, it was just another wild force of nature tamed. *I'll forever own a part of you now*, he told the waters.

As the only vehicle, it only took a few seconds to unload the ferry when they reached the other shore. The driver aimed the car west toward the massive tan desert that surrounded the narrow patch of the Nile's verdant riverbanks. The signs directing traffic to the Valley of the Kings were everywhere, and they followed them to a long road leading into deeper into the desert.

The driver broke the silence when they neared the end of the road. "Closed," he said emphatically, looking into the rearview mirror. He had already been paid handsomely to take Buchholz to the Valley of the Kings, but the driver still felt the need to warn him. "Closed," he repeated.

Buchholz nodded to show he understood the man, but gestured as he replied, "It's okay. Drop me off in the parking lot."

Duty fulfilled, the driver shrugged—if the crazy foreign actor wanted to go into the desert in the middle of the night, fine. He pulled into the empty lot and dropped Buchholz off. He was the guards' problem now.

Buchholz slowly approached the gate, unaccustomed to

walking in his shoes. By the time he was within the lamppost's circle of light, two men had exited the guard building. He was glad that their AK-103s were pointed down and they were using trigger discipline.

"What are you doing here?" the senior man called out in perfect English.

He followed the instructions and gave the proscribed response when challenged at the entrance. "I'm here to see Hor-Nebwy." He spoke in English, but the words he heard come out of his mouth were definitely not English, nor were they Arabic. They were something other…something older.

The guards' faces glazed over at the phrase and one answered in the same tongue. Much to his surprise, he understood the words perfectly. "Follow the path on the right and travel over the ridge. Perform the prayers there." Message delivered, they turned and walked, zombie-like, back into their quarters. Buchholz had no idea what kind of magic had just taken place, but he wished he had his saltcaster with him, just to see what kind of signature an ancient power gave off.

He skirted the gate and kept to the right. After five minutes, the lights from the parking lot dimmed into the background of the clear, cloudless night sky. He had no flashlight and instead used the sliver of the waning crescent moon coupled with starlight to find his way along the path. When it ran headlong into a wall of rock, it turned and continued parallel.

He didn't follow and instead scrambled up and over the

ridge in his questionable footwear, navigating the shifting sands on the other side. With all signs of habitation behind him, he looked westward. The world seemed much wilder here. There was nothing but sand and rock for the next two thousand five hundred miles, and it stared back at him, sizing him up—was he brave and cunning enough to cross?

Buchholz faced the vast wasteland and drew a rough circle around himself. He fell to his knees, closed his eyes, and bowed his head. *Ready or not…* he thought to himself before steadying his mind for the ritual composed in Demotic Egyptian. His lack of proficiency in the language would have been a problem if he was trying to cast a spell, as he simply didn't have the subtextual understanding of the language required to practice the arts in it. Luckily, he was only trying to get Hor-Nebwy's attention, not work any magic. All he had to do was say the right things pronounced closely enough, and the mummy would answer and open a path to the Valley of the Magi.

To help with that pronunciation, the Salt Mine had provided the litany using the International Phonetic Alphabet. Learning IPA was a bear for every new agent, but it was an essential skill, as precise pronunciation could prove the difference between life and death in their business. Instructions in IPA also prevented the average person from accidentally stumbling across something should the instructions ever get out—the IPA lexicon was used almost exclusively by linguists, and it looked like gibberish to everyone else. With effort, it could be deciphered by a layman, but it was an extra layer of protection nonetheless.

No musical tones had been included with the summoning instructions, meaning that the recitation didn't have a melodic component, so to ease his memorization, he'd looped it in his head to the main riff of Deep Purple's "Smoke on the Water." It was easy to remember and fit the syllables.

Hor-Nebwy was inspecting his valley when the supplication came through like a whisper on the wind. He attuned himself to the petitioner's voice—the words were technically correct, if stilted in pronunciation, but the melodic drone to which they were chanted grated against his proverbial ears. He sliced through the barriers between realms and found his supplicant, assuming a humble posture.

"That is enough," his dry voice ordered, and Buchholz obeyed without raising his forehead from the sand. "You are the Hobgoblin?"

Buchholz heard the command in English, but he doubted that was the language its speaker had employed. "I am Hobgoblin," he responded, face still down and eyes closed. His words were incomprehensible, but he knew what he was saying because he knew what he wanted to say. It was like listening to a recording of himself speaking a foreign language.

"Be still while Hator examines you," Hor-Nebwy instructed him. Seconds after the mummy spoke, Buchholz heard the first chuffing emanating from his left. He froze in place as the serpopard circled him, simultaneously sniffing with his cold nose as well as tasting the air around him as its forked tongue darted in and out of its mouth. He hoped all the scented oils he'd anointed himself with beforehand didn't whet the creature's appetite. Hator finished his scrutiny and vocalized loudly. Hor-Nebwy rubbed behind its ears.

"Rise and follow me," Hor-Nebwy bid his guest. Buchholz took to his feet and followed the gray skeletal figure and the snake-necked leopard to the rocky valley in the middle of a sea of sand. The unwrapped mummy was short, not even five-foot-six, and dressed in an ornately woven shendyt. His mummified feet were bare to the sand, and Buchholz was envious that he couldn't cast off his woven reed shoes. He stayed a respectable distance behind the pair, and the trio crossed several small dunes in silence until they bested a massive dune. Once crested, the Valley of the Magi came into view.

Two massive, flat-topped pillars loomed over the mouth of the valley. They shot high into the air, conical in shape and covered with layers of golden hieroglyphs along their entire length. The runes glowed in the night against the ebony columns. Buchholz could feel the power radiating from them even at this distance. The valley beyond was pock-marked with black rectangular spots; they were innumerable like the stars.

"This is the Valley of the Magi," Hor-Nebwy began. "This has been my home since the two Egypts were reunited by Khasekhemwy after the civil war. What you see before you looks like the Valley of the Kings, but this is the original and the Valley of the Kings the copy." He turned and faced Buchholz, who found it hard to focus on anything but the lines of the ancient being's face. It was like staring into a vast pool of time. Buchholz had to force himself to breathe. *In... Out... In... Out...*

Hor-Nebwy, pleased that the mortal was adequately awed, continued his grand exposition. "It is here that I record the lives of those interred and ensure that they live forever in the afterlife. It is a slow process, but there is nothing else of importance. Time passes and everything ends, but not here. Not against my will.

"For thousands of years, I have molded this land to be what yours can never be: permanent. Here, the past is never forgotten. The anger of your people, rooted in the knowledge that their span is short and pitiful, cannot express itself here. The statues are never defaced or shattered, and the rock will not succumb to the ravages of sand and wind.

"You can understand how a theft from this place is not just unacceptable, but insulting—not just to myself, but to all things that have lived and died," Hor-Nebwy said with ire.

It wasn't a question, and Buchholz wasn't sure how to answer. He stuck with a generic deep bow and uttered, "Great Hor-Nebwy, I am unworthy to offer any opinion on such things."

Buchholz felt the mummy's esoteric gaze fall on him,

peering deep into his soul. Hor-Nebwy said nothing, and Buchholz wondered if he'd answered wrong. He started to sweat in the cool desert night as the mummy stared at him. Unlike a living creature, Hor-Nebwy had no need to breathe or fidget, and once he stopped moving, he resembled a statue.

"You are missing something," the mummy finally spoke, stepping close enough to tap a dry finger tipped by a long brown nail upon Buchholz's chest. "Something that is here is not here."

His skin tingled where Hor-Nebwy made contact. "An amulet, Great Hor-Nebwy. I removed it to wear appropriate clothing," he answered humbly.

Hor-Nebwy grunted. "It smells interesting." He turned around and strode toward the valley, and it was understood that Buchholz should follow. He struggled to keep up the pace and he was breathless by the time they reached the conical pillars.

"Great Hor-Nebwy, may I pause to admire your great work?" he intoned between gasps of air.

The mummy paused at the request. "Of course. This must be very impressive to one of your station."

Buchholz caught his breath and cast his eyes upon the tapering pillars. The symbols were even more intricate up close, hypnotic in their pulsating brilliance as they graced the conical column. He didn't recognize many of them, and for the first time, he wished he was more of an academician. The higher he looked, the more distorted the runes became, but the lowest circle was clear to him. It was a centering ring. the first hollow magic circle that practitioners learned. When his brain got more oxygen, it dawned on him what he was looking at—the Valley of the Magi was protected by inset hollow magical circles.

Hollow magic circles were precise affairs. Each had to be perfect when created, and part of their perfection was the emptiness of their interior. It was generally accepted that there wasn't a way to put a circle within a circle without ruining the power of the exterior circle, but Buchholz was looking at a matryoshka doll of hollow magic circles, achieved by using the taper of the pillar. Hor-Nebwy had engraved row upon row of hollow magic circles. Buchholz imagined the raw amount of power that could be wielded from the top of the pillar, surrounded by more than a dozen circles at one.

Hor-Nebwy knew the hearts of men and spoke cautionary words. "You will die if you stand on the obelisk. You do not have the mastery for it. Perhaps your master does, but she is not the kind to take such personal risks."

"Yes, Great Hor-Nebwy. I will take your warning to heart," Buchholz replied and guarded his thoughts more closely.

"We don't have much farther to go," Hor-Nebwy announced as he resumed walking. They traveled along the length of the valley, where its shoulders closed in around them. The mummy pointed at a tomb opening far up the cliff. "We are nearly there," he gravelly rumbled. Hator waited dutifully at the bottom of the ramp as they ascended along the narrow path that turned back on itself numerous times on the way up.

On the ascent, Buchholz noticed something odd in the sand that lightly covered the path—a set of tracks four inches wide and eighteen inches apart. He was careful to avoid stepping on them, but Hor-Nebwy paid no mind, striding with purpose up the slope and stopping in front of a tomb entrance.

"This is where the theft occurred," Hor-Nebwy informed him.

"Great Hor-Nebwy, may I ask what has been stolen?" Buchholz deferentially inquired.

Hor-Nebwy's face tightened, which Buchholz didn't think was possible given the state of body. "Someone has taken Mau."

Buchholz kept his face and thoughts completely still; he may not have heard of Hor-Nebwy up until a few days ago, but even he had heard the tales of Mau the cat. It was despicable to steal a guy's cat, but Mau wasn't a run of the mill kitty. She was a feline of legend, and there was no place on earth she could not go. She was the ultimate infiltrator, and whoever had her now was her master.

"Great Hor-Nebwy, that is truly a grave insult. You have called for me and I have come, but I am a lowly peon. Why have you bestowed such an honor upon me?" Buchholz laid it on as thick as possible.

"I know the ways of the Land of the Dead. You have sent many there, and I need such a mighty warrior to capture and punish the thief. There will be no mercy to one who steals from the Valley of the Magi." Hor-Nebwy spoke with righteous anger.

Buchholz bowed at the compliment—he was good at his job. "What of this, Great Hor-Nebwy?" he said, pointing to the path.

Hor-Nebwy bent down to the patch of ground and turned his preternatural sight on it. His skin crackled with the movement. "That is sand," he declared authoritatively.

Buchholz pressed cautiously and took a knee beside the tracks. "Forgive my lack of clarity, Great Hor-Nebwy. I mean these marks. I am curious what has made them? They do not resemble your steps, nor that of your guardians."

The mummy stared at the sand but saw nothing unusual. *Can it be the mortal sees something I cannot?* He jumped into the Hobgoblin and saw through his eyes.

Buchholz reeled back as his consciousness was pulled out of his body to make space for the ancient power. The jarring force felt like a parachute opening during a head-first dive in the pitch black of a moonless night—he was glad to no longer be in freefall, but had no idea where he'd land. He watched his body touch the sand, rub it between his fingers, and trace the trajectory of the track marks. Just as suddenly as he was displaced, Buchholz fell back into his body. He caught himself with his left arm, inches away from smashing his face against the sand.

"It appears you are correct," Hor-Nebwy conceded. "I have chosen wisely."

Chapter Nine

Luxor, Egypt
27th of October, 5:05 p.m. (GMT+2)

Buchholz was floating in nothingness, blackness all around him. He didn't know how long he had been there, but there was a constant beat marking time. It was steady and persistent, and he started to count them, hoping it would orient him in this nebulous space. Somewhere around two hundred, he realized it was his heartbeat. *I'm alive…that's good*, he thought to himself.

He saw nothing, which he found remarkably comforting. It was better than watching his body from the outside. In the background, other noises started to seep through: footsteps, voices, the squeak of doors, and wheels in need of lubrication. He was lying down on something soft and smooth, definitely not the sandy ground of the Valley of the Magi. Buchholz seriously doubted Hor-Nebwy would have bothered to slip a pillow under his head.

His eyelids fluttered as he tried to will them open and see what awaited him. Eventually, the muscles obeyed their master, and he winced at the bright fluorescents overhead. He had been in darkness long enough that the light stung a little. A figure moved over him, blocking out the worst of it.

"Nalin?" A soft feminine voice spoke with care. A face came into focus as his eyes adjusted: the perfectly proportioned heart-shaped visage of Alicia Elspeth Hovdenak Moncrief— codename Clover. Her blue eyes were tired, her blonde hair thrown back into a messy bun, and her clothes were rumpled. Even in this uncharacteristically untidy state, she was a sight for sore eyes,

"Alicia?" he tested his voice. It was strained and scratchy but still his. "Where am I?"

"You're in El Qornaa Central Hospital in Luxor," she answered and poured some water into a cup with a straw. She held the straw to his lips. "Little sips," she prompted.

His parched throat demanded more after the first drops made contact, but there was only so much he could take in without choking. "What time...what *day* is it?" he asked, taking note of the tubes attached to him. An IV bag dripped into his left arm and he had a nasal cannula blowing oxygen into his nostrils.

"It's the twenty-seventh of October, late afternoon," she replied. "They found you three days ago in the desert, nearly dead from dehydration and raving about a mummy trying to take over your body."

"There weren't any explosions? That doesn't sound like me at all," he instinctively joked while he fished around for the controls to raise the head of the bed—he was quite at home in hospitals. "Three days gone? That's one hell of a case of dehydration."

Moncrief smirked at his cavalier attitude in the face of death. She'd salted and run her will over him numerous times since she arrived; he'd definitely had a run-in with something, but it appeared he was still very much Hobgoblin. "The doctors said it was a miracle you were even alive—by all rights, you should be at the morgue instead of the hospital." She handed him the controls dangling over the rail.

He pushed himself up onto his elbows, adjusted the bed, and strove to sit up. He was a little winded after the maneuver, eliciting Moncrief's assistance and concern. "You feeling okay?"

Buchholz did a quick assessment, physically and mentally. "Tired. Drawn out. Got a grade-A headache. Otherwise, everything else seems fine." He pulled out the tube from his nostrils, and started unhooking himself from the monitors. "You didn't happen to bring me something to wear, did you?" He didn't relish the thought of walking out of here in a shendyt.

"I brought you some real clothes," she teased him, pulling out a suit and shoes from the open wardrobe. She'd had a good laugh when the hospital showed her what he was wearing when he was brought in. "They didn't know what to make of what you were wearing, so I told them you were an actor."

"Given my situation, I must be very method then," he quipped as he pulled the IV from his peripheral vein with one smooth motion. It was only a matter of time before someone noticed the absence of vitals on the monitor and checked up on him. "When can we leave?"

"I've had the plane ready to go ever since I landed."

"Good," he replied, taking off his clothes. "I've got work to do." He grabbed the starched shirt and started getting dressed. Buchholz made no attempt at modesty, and Moncrief was never one to shy away from the nude form, especially one as fetching as his. Hobgoblin was always nice to look at; the problems usually started after he opened his mouth. "I'm already three days behind."

Moncrief watched him intently as he pulled up his slacks and wound the belt through the loops. *What a very un-Hobgoblin thing to say.* "So quick to get back…are you sure you are feeling all right?"

He bent down and tied his shoes. His feet still remembered where the woven reed slippers rubbed them wrong. He gave her a dashing smile when he came back up. "I was made an offer I couldn't refuse," he said in his best Brando impression. He flipped up his collar, and his hands whipped the tie into a perfect Windsor knot. "Plus, what I really need now is some specialized rehydration from your on-board supplies," he made reference to the fully stocked bar on her private jet.

"Pretty sure that's not medically advised," she said dubiously.

"Well, I'm already checking myself out AMA, so… *wenn schon, denn schon,*" he reasoned as he gave himself the once over in the mirror. It was no surprise that the suit fit him like a glove. Moncrief had all their measurements for outfits specialized for esoteric purposes, but it also came in handy when she flew into town to support or rescue an agent.

He addressed Moncrief's reflection in the mirror, "All right, let's retrieve my stuff from the hotel and get out of here." Moncrief let down her hair and donned her heiress demeanor. It was the poise that came with good breeding and one that took umbrage when questioned. It was the steely hardness behind the smiles and dimples that informed everyone that Hobgoblin was leaving the hospital, no questions asked.

Buchholz didn't mind the assumptions people made when he traveled with Moncrief—he was pretty and didn't everyone like a little arm candy? Since everyone was assuming it anyway, he played the part of a frivolous actor who took his craft too seriously until they were safely in the air, headed back to Detroit.

The quiet roar of the twin Rolls-Royce turbofans faded into the background as Buchholz rapidly typed composed an update to Leader. They would be speaking face-to-face soon enough, but he knew she would want to know about Mau as soon as possible. There was nowhere the cat couldn't go, including the Salt Mine.

As he typed out the update, it felt like working through a haze. His mind had been scrambled, not just from the mummy jumping into his body to obtain mortal sensory input, but his memories were also out of sorts. Certain things were crystal-clear, like the tracks in the sand and the scene of the theft, while others were fuzzy and disjointed, like a radio station beyond its signal area. Disjointed bits and pieces blinked into view, but the parts between them were either entirely missing or sped up much too fast to make out any detail. It made sense why there was so little information about the Valley of the Magi—Hor-Nebwy guarded its secrets jealously.

At Moncrief's insistence, he ate something before he had his second immaculate Gimlet made with Plymouth Navy Strength. She traveled with a kitchen, bedroom, and full bath, and the entourage all that required. Her staff were skilled, loyal, and discreet, and they took each of Ms. Moncrief's guests in stride.

Buchholz wolfed down dinner: steak with whipped potatoes and asparagus. He had no idea where they'd obtained such tender stalks out of season, but such was the life of an heiress. It was his first real food in days and would have tasted heavenly, even if it wasn't prepared by a master chef. Moncrief let him eat in peace and didn't begin her probing until he was digging into dessert. "So?" she said innocently.

He looked up from his parfait. "Yes?"

"Aren't you going to tell me what happened?" she nudged.

He played his cards close to his chest. "I went into the desert, came back out alive, and now I'm here with you. The end."

Moncrief took her spoon out of her dessert and pointed it at him. "Nice try. Spill, Hobgoblin."

"What did Leader tell you?" he coyly asked.

"That's not fair. She's always close-mouthed," she countered.

"I'm not sure I should say anything," he strung her along. "You know how she is. But, I suppose you'll know eventually…"

Moncrief was insulted at his attempt to play a game she had championed long ago. She sat back and feigned disinterest. She dipped her spoon back into her parfait. "It's a pity we aren't sharing, because I can't tell you mine if you won't tell me yours."

Buchholz grinned. "What could you possible tell me about my own case that I don't already know?"

Moncrief's chest bounced slightly as she shrugged her slim shoulders. "Did you know you were summoned by an exploding corpse?" She placed a small bite in her mouth and savored the sharp fresh raspberry against the whipped cream and bits of crumble amidst the silky custard.

He looked sideways at her and calculated. "You're bluffing."

"That's fine. I can wait," she insisted graciously. "If Leader calls a meeting, I'll know yours soon enough." She paused to take another bite. "But will you know mine? I mean, you've already been to the desert and back."

Buchholz waved his white linen napkin in surrender. "Fine, you win. Tell me about the exploding corpse. You know you're dying to."

Moncrief pounced on the offer. "So, this guy who'd been dead for about a week showed up on the bridge to Zug, demanding to see Leader."

"Seriously?" Buchholz said in disbelief. "That's like kicking a fire ant's nest." Then again, Hor-Nebwy didn't do subtle.

"Right? It triggered a dozen different alarms, and I heard it almost came to blows until LaSalle showed up," she said conspiratorially.

"Heard from who?" he grilled her.

She flippantly waved her hand and declared, "Not important. What is interesting is that LaSalle figured out the guy was actually possessed by some other being. It insisted on speaking directly to Leader, and LaSalle decided to bring it into the Mine because there was no way he was going have her come out to meet it."

"Wait," he interjected, "if they brought it inside, that means it got through the Process." The Process was a magical gauntlet the Mine had created to reveal and hedge out malicious magics. Every agent eventually went through it, as their loyalty would come into question at some point due to all the strange or powerful supernatural things they came into contact with. For an agent, clearing the Process meant they were free from exterior control. Buchholz took another sip of his drink at the thought of the mummy's reach. *How could Hor-Nebwy maintain possession of a body through that?*

"I know, wild," she blithely pressed on with her narrative. "So they get the corpse down into the Mine, run it through the Process, and somehow the necromantic connection held. It gets its private meeting with Leader. Once the conversation was over, it keeled over and gassed off. Made a huge mess."

Buchholz nodded his head. "It tracks. Leader did smell like a walking bleach advertisement when she briefed me."

"So you want to tell me who jacked you up and left you in the desert to die?" Moncrief asked bluntly.

For a second, Buchholz wondered if saying his name would somehow draw his attention, but shook himself free of the thought. This wasn't some children's book, and he was already on the mummy's arcane radar. "Hor-Nebwy."

Moncrief reflexively thwacked his arm. "Shut up. Are you fucking with me?"

"You know him?" he said quizzically.

"By reputation," she qualified. "My maternal grandparents were big Egyptophiles. He's old school magic in the truest sense of the word. I can't believe you've actually met him. What's he like?"

Buchholz's face darkened as he found himself struggling to elegantly sum up the shreds of memory he had of his exposure to the ancient mummy. "Powerful and used to getting his own way," he started. "Unpleasant, with no regard for anyone else. Even though he summoned me, I didn't matter to him at all. Who calls a human out to the desert and doesn't think about how much they need water to live?"

"It's possible his magic was what kept you alive until help arrived. I picked up a signature on you when I first got to Luxor," she said gently.

"If he did, it's only because he wants my help finding lost property and punishing the thief," he scoffed bitterly. "I mean, even a demon finds something of value with you, something that it'll enjoy breaking. Hor-Nebwy is just monumentally indifferent, but in a dangerous way. It's like being in a cage with a well-fed tiger. You know there's no reason for it to hurt you, but you never really know what passes for reason with the tiger, do you? So you're bound to it, lurking only a few feet away, just waiting for it to look at you in that particular way."

Moncrief touched his arm, physically grounding him to the here and now. "You're not there anymore. We'll get you back to the Mine, you do the job, and you're done. Just like every mission before."

Buchholz followed her words back to the present and brushed off his gloom with a laugh. "Yeah. You're right."

"Of course I'm right." She removed her hand and gave him a smile. "Now finish your dessert. It's delicious."

He moved his spoon around, muddling the crisp layers until it was more a homogenous goo than a parfait. His dinner had caught up with him, and he was already fuller than was comfortable. He went over Moncrief's account again and his twisted mind found the humor in it on the second time around. "Can you imagine Leader's face right after the corpse exploded?"

Moncrief smirked. "I would have loved to be a fly on that wall."

"Poor LaSalle!" he blurted out. LaSalle hated getting wrinkles on his clothes, much less decaying chunks.

Moncrief mimicked Leader's commanding tone, "David, could you come in here for a moment? I need your assistance." Buchholz did not expect to laugh so hard at her spot-on imitation and couldn't stop himself from snorting repeatedly, which only fed Moncrief's mirth.

Like a camera going off, her radiant face and golden hair framed against the blackness of the window behind her suddenly etched itself into his memory. He felt the night trying to creep into the cabin. It wasn't enough that it had claimed all of the sky; it wanted to invade their tiny sliver of metal floating thirty-six thousand feet above the earth. It pressed against the hull; it wanted inside.

Somewhere in his own internal inky blackness, he heard his voice repeat familiar words. *I'll forever own a part of you now. Time passes and everything ends.*

Chapter Ten

Detroit, Michigan, USA
28th of October, 6:45 a.m. (GMT-4)

The racing bass rift dragged Buchholz from his slumber, and he groped blindly for his phone. Lemmy had just declared he didn't want to live forever when he finally swiped his alarm off. "You and me both, brother," he groaned, falling back on his pillow. The thought of stealing a few more minutes of sleep crossed his mind, but in a moment of what felt like heroic discipline, he pushed the heavy comforter off his naked body and let the cold do the rest. He had places to be.

He pulled a plush robe from his closet to keep the chill at bay while he stumbled to the kitchen and wildly opened cabinets and drawers until he had everything he needed for coffee. Normally, he would have his first cup after he showered, but it felt like he wasn't even going to make it to the bathroom without a pick-me-up. While he waited for the brew, he stared out the window. It was still dark and would be for at least another hour. Across the river, Windsor, Ontario looked like a miniature city from his twentieth-story apartment.

This place was all his, but he didn't spend much time here. He generally preferred warmer climes, especially in winter. It basically served as a permanent way station between missions as well as storage for the few possessions he'd kept from his old life. It was tastefully furnished because he liked nice things, but in a functional way. This was his flat, not his home.

Buchholz yawned and stretched as he waited. When he'd stepped into Moncrief's G650, he'd been shagged out, like he always was after action, but he knew it would pass quickly and sleep was the best remedy. The body did some of its best work at flushing the special evolutionary cocktail it generated under stress when it had nothing else to do but rest. He'd caught a few hours of sleep on the plane, but his circadian rhythm was shot to hell between the jetlag and the hospital, and when he rolled into his apartment a little after midnight, he'd popped a pill to help him sleep. He was mentally adding up all the hours he'd spent in some state of unconsciousness in the past five days when the click of the coffee machine ended his calculations— his go juice was done.

With the first cup down, he set up the machine for a second and got ready. Not long after he sent the message about Mau, Leader had elected to debrief him over the phone. He could tell she was disappointed that he couldn't remember more, but also not surprised. When his and Moncrief's phones simultaneously alerted them to an all-hands meeting minutes later, he figured it was serious, but not world ending. His scale of danger and doom had drastically reset during his time with the Salt Mine.

He felt like a new man after he stepped out of the shower,

and he contemplated food over his second cup of coffee. The meeting started at nine, and he knew a diner that did a servable fried hash not far from the Springwells exit nearest Zug Island. With breakfast in his sights, he hurriedly dressed and pulled his custom WRX out of its parking spot. Once he was clear of the parking lot, he turned up the volume, letting the music push against the Detroit morning gloom.

The diner was a holdover from another age, and it was an age that suited him well. There weren't many places like it left outside of Michigan—a greasy spoon that didn't feel the need to pretend it was anything else. The ding of an actual bell rang every time the door opened, and the coffee was hot, fresh, and cheap. They served breakfast all day, and everyone minded their business. He took a seat at the far end of the counter after sweeping the clientele to make sure no one stood out as too unusual. A sweet but sassy waitress took his order, eying him up from behind her glasses. He took it in stride and pretended not to notice.

While he didn't have any more memories of his time with Hor-Nebwy, he had pieced together a timeline from what Moncrief and the Egyptian doctors had told him. He'd spent the better part of a day and a night walking the Valley of the Magi, presumably entertaining the mummy's novelty of observing his work through mortal senses. Buchholz didn't have the time or inclination to unpack that experience, but his immediate takeaway was to be better prepared the next time he entered the valley. Once the mummy had his cat back, Buchholz would no longer be needed, and Hor-Nebwy could be even more indifferent to the needs of a transient human.

His meal arrived fast and hot, and he hungrily shoved the corned beef hash into his mouth, soaking up the grease and runny egg yolk with the rye toast that came on the side. The hash browns were just the right kind of crispy, almost burnt but not quite. He didn't normally eat this sort of thing—he didn't get his body eating that many carbs or calories—which only made it more glorious when he did. It was his treat for surviving.

Not many people could handle being an operative, much less a supernatural one. Training helped, but in his opinion, someone either had it or they didn't. A person could only will themselves to tough it out so far before they tapped out. You had to rebound quickly when you took a beating. You had to be able to bend to the point of breaking, and when you did finally snap—*everyone* snapped—you had to knit yourself back together again. Short of that, don't bother. Be an accountant.

He dropped his fork and pushed his plate away—it had almost defeated him and to eat more would be unwise, even if the cherry pie in the pie case was calling his name. He left enough cash under his empty cup to cover the bill and a generous tip, and the bell dinged as he opened the door and made his exit. It was a short drive to Zug Island and, as always, he backed his car into a parking spot. He wondered who would make the meeting today as he matched vehicles to their drivers. He didn't recognize the colorful 718 Boxter parked opposite him, but he whistled in appreciation when he saw its driver climb out.

"Got a new one, huh?" he hailed her.

Moncrief grabbed her purse and locked up her latest toy. "I didn't have one in lava orange," she said flippantly, making no attempt to dim the wide grin on her face. Driving to Zug Island was one of the few times she got to drive herself around, and she liked the taste of freedom that came with being behind the wheel. She gave him a polite nod as he held the elevator for her. "Any idea what Leader's cooking up?"

Buchholz presented his titanium key and they descended to the first floor of the Salt Mine. "My lips are sealed—don't want to take the thunder out of her meeting."

She lips leveled flat. "You really know how to disappoint a lady," she jabbed.

"One of my many skills," he snidely rolled with the punches and smiled at her reflection in the elevator doors that were just starting to open.

"Honed through years of practice, I'm sure," she added drily.

"Decades," Buchholz bantered back. Her high-pitched laugh erupted out of the elevator.

"You two are in high spirits today," the metallic voice of Angela Abrams crackled through the old speaker.

"Any day you're alive is a good day," Buchholz cheerily greeted her as he deposited his possession for the security check. He dramatically raised an eyebrow. "You staying blonde? Because it suits you," he complimented her.

Abrams gave him a smile and waved him through once the sensor beeped. Moncrief, however, did not get off so easily—Abrams regaled her with talks of what she and her latest beau had done this weekend. Clover smiled and nodded; she only had herself to blame—when she forgot to activate her resting bitch face, she looked entirely too approachable.

Once it was confirmed that they weren't carrying anything dangerous or untoward into the Salt Mine, they made their way to the fourth floor with minutes to spare. It was quite a turn out. Leader, severe and gray, sat at the head of the table with David LaSalle, calm and restrained, never far away. Teresa Martinez, codename Lancer, was brown and beautiful as ever, and locked in friendly conversation with Joan Liu, codename Aurora, who was casual yet deadly. Recently resurrected from a deep cover, Aaron Haddock, codename Stigma, was shooting the breeze with Clarence Morris, codename Deacon. Only Prism was missing. He hadn't seen her in a long time.

Deacon's face lit up when he saw Hobgoblin enter the room. His booming voice greeted Buchholz with equal parts affection and chiding. "Boy, what's this I hear about you wandering the desert—didn't I teach you better than that?"

"Don't start with me, old man. I know for a fact you've

wandered sketchier places than that," he said suggestively. Deacon laughed and they hugged; it had been months since they had seen each other. When Buchholz first joined the Salt Mine, Deacon trained him, and even though that was ages ago, he had a deep affection for the old coot.

Deacon was black as night and battered around the edges, but he was always impeccably dressed, although never gaudy or flashy. He didn't look like much, but there was a grizzled charisma about him. He had seen things, done things, and knew things, so it wasn't worth trying to pull a fast one on him. And when he spoke with authority, it was like hearing the voice of God, if one believed in that sort of thing. If he told you night was day and up was down, you'd want to believe him. Buchholz only wished he was as good with the ladies as Deacon had been in his day, something which the old man had repeatedly reminded him of during his training period. They had made an odd couple on paper, but they'd been a great team once upon a time and both were a little sad when it came time for Hobgoblin to start working on his own.

Leader cleared her voice and the room quieted. "Now that Hobgoblin's here, we can begin." LaSalle went around the table, handing out identical folders to each of the agents while she began the meeting. "Last week, the Salt Mine received a visitation request from an unusual source: Hor-Nebwy, the ancient mummy practitioner that maintains the Valley of the Magi. At the time, he was tight-lipped about the details, but after meeting with Hobgoblin, we have a fuller picture of his situation. Someone has stolen Mau."

"Mau, as in the cat who can walk through walls, Mau?" Liu asked.

"The very one," Leader affirmed. "She is now out of Hor-Nebwy's control and whoever has her mummified form is calling the shots. There is no security that can keep her out and anything is ripe for theft."

"Do we know how long she's been missing?" Lancer inquired.

"Nothing concrete," Leader admitted, "but the last time Hor-Nebwy used Mau was a little more than a year ago. It could have been any time after that."

"I thought the Valley of the Magi was impenetrable. How could anyone have gotten in?" Clover chimed in.

Leader turned the floor over to Hobgoblin. "The valley is extensively warded, which leads me to believe it was not directly breeched by a supernatural creature or practitioner of the arts. There was a set of tracks leading to the tomb Mau was held in, so it's possible someone used a remote-controlled vehicle to retrieve Mau. It could be a way of bypassing the wards. It's possible that Hor-Nebwy isn't current enough with modern technology to be guarding against such intrusions."

"That would mean the thief not only knew about the Valley of the Magi, but also knew the location of Mau's mummy," Stigma reasoned. The room mulled over that one for a while.

Leader picked up the narrative in the lull. "In your files, you'll find basic information about Mau and Hor-Nebwy, as well as a list of possibly related thefts identified by our analysts. As you can see, the list is long and geographically diverse. Until we have more concrete information to narrow down the list, we are doing this the old-fashioned way.

"When you read the case files, familiarize yourself with all of the robberies, not just the sites you've been individually assigned. LaSalle has created a secure group message—report your findings there instead of directly to me. We need a free flow of information as it becomes available. The sooner Mau is back with its rightful owner, the better.

"Right now Chloe, Dot, and Weber are doing a thorough inventory of the Mine's holding cells to make sure we're not leaking items, and we have set up wards to alert us to trans-dimensional visitors. They won't stop Mau from entering, but at least we would know if she comes. Each of you should also review your own private sanctuaries. Particularly you, Clover."

Moncrief curtly nodded—message received.

"Hobgoblin is lead, so provide him with as much assistance as possible. Clover, you're teamed with Hobgoblin—he's going to need enhanced mobility, and there are some high profile thefts that are going to need your connections to gain audience to some of the crime scenes."

Leader paused briefly to see if anyone had questions, and when none seemed forthcoming, she finished the meeting with a final consideration. "I want to draw your attention to a particular quirk about Mau. Even though she is a legend in her own right, she doesn't leave a magical signature. Mau functions as an extension of the will of her master, so if Mau's master is a practitioner, their signature should be picked up by saltcasting."

"So it's possible the new master may not be a practitioner?" Deacon posited.

"We don't know anything for certain yet, so the lack of a pattern at a crime scene doesn't necessarily rule out Mau's involvement in a theft at this point in time," Leader clarified. The weight of the daunting task ahead hung heavy over the agents of the Salt Mine as Leader dismissed them, turning them loose to catch a thief.

Chapter Eleven

Detroit, Michigan, USA
28th of October, 10:20 a.m. (GMT-4)

Buchholz unlocked the door to his penthouse apartment in the Asher Building, one of the many riverfront steel and glass towers built in the past twenty years to revitalize Detroit. He tossed his keys into the bowl that sat on the entryway table. "This is it," he announced to Moncrief as she followed him in. "Make yourself at home. Can I get you anything to drink?" he offered as he secured the door behind her.

"No, thank you," she replied graciously, taking in his living room. It was the quintessential expression of masculinity in shades of gray, plus or minus a hint of hunter green or gunpowder blue. The furnishings were clean and crisp in strong, stark lines, and there was nary a throw pillow in sight. The bearskin rug in front of the fireplace held no sense of irony, and the sparse art was modern in sensibility with an overabundance of the naked female form in paint and sculpture.

She wandered to the bank of windows overlooking the river while Buchholz sifted through his mail, checking for things of importance before adding it to the rest of the mailers that that hadn't yet made their way to the recycling bin. "Curious to see how the other half lives?" he teased at her wandering gaze.

"You think a riverfront penthouse apartment is the other half?" she pertly challenged him.

"To an heiress, this is downright the sticks," he cracked wise, heading for the bedroom. "I won't be long—just have to check my things and repack my suitcase." He closed the door behind him before approaching the reproduction of Hans Breinlinger's *Zwei Unheimliche* hanging on the wall. He ran his hand along the backside of the frame, feeling for the lever. The print swung on its hinge once he released the latch and he turned the dial.

Buchholz's stash was largely mundane in nature: passports, currency, explosives, detonators, and backup weapons. Most of his magical armory was issued by Weber and carried on his person when he was on the job, except for his fish amulet and a few other odd bits he'd picked up over the years. He had the obligatory backup stash of magical bullets for different regions—some people took home office supplies from work, he siphoned banishment bullets. Once he was certain nothing was missing, he repacked his gear and clothing, and locked everything up again.

When he exited his bedroom, he found Moncrief in front of the ornate barrister bookcase with its rolling smoky glass cover up. She made no apologies or excuses for her snooping. Instead, she grabbed a title from the stacks. "Oh Hobgoblin, I would have never guessed," she taunted him. "Nancy Drew and her strawberry blonde hair?"

His face grew very serious. "Be careful with that," he urged her. "It's a first edition with the original Russell Tandy dust jacket intact." He gingerly took *The Sign of the Twisted Candles* back and returned it to its place. "It's my most recent acquisition. Cost a pretty penny, but now I have numbers one through fifty-three in first edition. Also, she wasn't strawberry blonde until there was a printing error in the 1950s and they ran with it."

Moncrief had an enigmatic look on her face; of all the guilty pleasures she could think of, this one didn't even register. "Hey, I get it. Everyone has their thing, and yours is teen girl detectives," she said neutrally as he closed the front with care.

He shrugged. "My grandmother had the whole series and used to read them to me to help me with my English. When I read them again, it reminds me of her."

Moncrief huffed and rolled her eyes. "Well, now you just look sweet, and I'm a jerk for giving you a hard time."

"I promise to make plenty of snide remarks when we get to your place," he sniped as he grabbed his special Weber-issued suitcase. "Let's go. I'm anxious to see Lifestyles of the Rich and Judgy, Moncrief Edition."

"You've never been over?" she said incredulously. Who hadn't been to her house?

"Never received a golden ticket," he chided.

She put on a stern face. "No falling into my chocolate river,

Mr. Gloop. I just had it cleaned."

Buchholz left his car at his apartment and jumped into Moncrief's, thinking it foolish to leave his car in long-term parking at the airport. He questioned his decision as he white-knuckled the ride. She liked to drive fast and aggressive, which was also his style but he was typically the one behind the wheel and it wasn't so fun from the passenger seat. He wouldn't go so far as to call her a bad driver, but she had an innate belief that everyone on the road should know where she wanted to go and get out of the way.

It was a short flight to Baltimore, Maryland, ninety minutes at most. When they boarded her G650, her faithful steward, Jeffery, had everything cleaned, restocked, and ready for takeoff. He even had a gimlet ready for Buchholz. He took objection to the assumption that he was a day drinker, but he had to admit, it was a good gimlet.

Moncrief made arrangements for their upcoming travel while Buchholz enjoyed his drink. They taxied forever as the call tower kept changing their slot, and both agents started reviewing the hefty briefing. Buchholz skimmed the background information and found nothing new in the entries concerning Hor-Nebwy and the Valley of the Magi, but he was interested to suss out fact from fiction on Mau.

Mau was actually the pet of Hor-Nebwy when he was pharaoh. She was an Egyptian Mau by breed, a rarity in modern times and generally considered one of the progenitor breeds of the modern domestic cat. Illustrations depict her with a short black coat, green eyes, and a lean muscular body with longer hind legs, which lent itself to the classic Egyptian silhouette of a cat.

When Hor-Nebwy returned to unlife as a mummy, he longed for a companion in the afterlife. Thus, he brought back the soul of Mau, put it into a living cat, and then killed and mummified it to keep him company. Up until her theft—*Or would it be an abduction?* Buchholz briefly pondered—Mau had resided in Hor-Nebwy's private tomb either in mummy form or as a black cat. Buchholz shook his head in disbelief. *That guy really loves his cat.*

There was plenty of conjecture and speculation about Mau's magical abilities, but the librarians confirmed that she could circumvent magical protections through unknown mechanisms. It was also documented that while Mau preferred her cat size, she was able to grow considerably larger if necessary. *I wonder how they know that*, Buchholz thought wryly, imaging a King Kong-sized black cat standing on her hind legs, batting at planes.

He looked up from his reading and threw out a hypothetical. "Are you a cat or dog person?"

"Whatever can feed itself and take care of its own waste," she answered without giving it a second thought.

"That pretty much rules out all pets," he observed.

"Which is why I don't have any," she replied with a tilt of

her head. "Have you had a chance to look at the robberies?"

"Just about to. Why?"

"It's weird. They are almost all art-related, but none of them are from institutions."

Buchholz nodded. "Smart. Private owners usually have a lot less security in place than galleries or museums, and if you have a fence, it's not hard to move art. Collectors aren't the sort to ask a lot of questions, especially those looking for a bargain."

"How good are you on your art?" Moncrief raised an eyebrow.

"Enough to sound knowledgeable to tipsy women at galas and gallery openings," he replied.

Moncrief shook her head. "Okay, you start brushing up on artists and stolen works from the thefts assigned to us, and I'll try to pick the lowest hanging fruit."

Chapter Twelve

Baltimore, Maryland, USA
28th of October, 1:05 p.m. (GMT-4)

"You seem to be doing well for yourself," Buchholz dryly remarked as the camphorwood paneled doors closed behind him. He'd never been in a private residence featuring a twelve-car underground garage and a private elevator.

"One does one's best," Moncrief undercut her circumstances in a vain attempt at modesty.

"When you said you lived in an old part of Baltimore, I didn't think you meant Mount Vernon Place. I'm pretty sure I could throw a stone and hit the Washington Monument from your roof," he speculated.

"Please don't—it would disrupt the neighbors to no end," she drolly replied.

When the elevator doors opened, the immaculately suited form of her long-time butler was there to greet her. "Welcome home, Miss. Your chamber is being prepared, as is the Agnew Room for your guest." Gerard was an older man whose nearly white hair had surrendered to encroaching baldness years ago, but there was an unmistakable pride in his appearance.

"Thank you, Gerard. The bags are in the car. Be a dear and

take care of those as well," she intoned blithely as she entered the grand foyer. Her heels clicked on the white marble floor speckled in gold and veined in green, and her voice echoed through all three floors. The wood paneling of the entryway softened the gleaming light that flooded in from the skylight and windows. "And tea?"

"Ready in forty-five minutes, Miss," Gerard answered, following a few steps behind and to the side of Moncrief.

"We'll wait in the music room, Gerard," she said with a perfunctory smile. *To the manor born*, thought Buchholz as they crossed the foyer.

"Very well. Shall Miss require refreshments?" the butler inquired.

"Nothing for me, Gerard," Moncrief replied and raised an eye toward Buchholz. "Would you care for anything to drink?"

"Sparking water would be lovely," he answered Moncrief. He had hobnobbed with enough wealthy people to know it was gauche to speak directly to the help if the host was present.

"As Sir wishes," Gerard replied and walked to the back of the house.

"The Agnew Room? As in Spiro Agnew?" Buchholz whispered once the butler had disappeared.

"The one and only," she confirmed. "He was a big name in Baltimore politics, and my grandparents were close friends of his before he went off to Washington."

"Do you have a Kennedy room?" he inquired facetiously.

"Don't be silly…that's at our summer home in Martha's Vineyard," she corrected him. He couldn't tell if she was serious, joking, or playfully telling the truth. "Extended hospitality is one old-world sensibility that survived the crossing of the Atlantic. It wasn't unusual for someone to stay for weeks at a time. Grand houses and families die if they don't have company."

"And you are just now getting around to inviting me," he feigned insult.

"It's not like you ever invited me to stay at your place," she countered. Before he could respond, she opened the door and announced. "The music room." It was large. If the seating was rearranged, there would be space enough for an intimate gathering with thirty of your closest friends for an evening of music. The walls were fully paneled exclusively in coffers, and the top row was carved in a running scene. The decorated plaster ceiling offset the rich hue of the wood, and a sparkling chandelier hung in the center of the room. It contained a menagerie of musical instruments, including a harp, a Chinese zither, and two pianos—one antique that was more for decoration and a shiny black Yamaha concert grand for playing. A large banded chest held a sundry of smaller instruments that made merry but didn't warrant presentation. Along one wall was a long bookshelf filled with sheet music, as well as biographies of the greater classical composers. The large fireplace was decidedly Victorian in design but the coffee table, chairs, and couch in front of it were more modern. It was almost too much to visually take in at once.

"Do you play any of these instruments?" he asked as he ran his finger along the edge of the grand—not even a speck of dust.

"A failed flute player and I'm passable on the piano, but my mother was the real musician," she answered. Her face softened at a long gone memory, and it left as suddenly as it came. "Why, do you play?" she changed the subject.

He took a seat at the bench. "Does chopsticks count?" he said with sincere eyes but a deadpan voice.

"I should think not, but I'm not a musician," she qualified.

"I can also play the first four bars of Foreigner's 'Cold as Ice,'" he added optimistically, as if it would make a difference.

"Well, that changes everything! You should have led with that," she advised sardonically. "I'll gladly give you the grand tour of the house, but I was hoping to check my collection first. With any luck, I'll be done in time to meet you for tea in the breakfast room. Do you think you can entertain yourself in here in the meantime?"

Buchholz nodded. "Don't worry about me. I'll find some way to amuse myself."

"Gerard should be by with your water shortly, and he'll retrieve you for tea," she subtly informed him; there was no need for him to bumble his way through the first floor looking for the breakfast room.

Moncrief heard the first bars of chopsticks as she left the room and passed Gerard in the foyer on her way to the family vault. The entrance was in the basement of the mansion, accessible only via the stairwell in the kitchen. Near the stairs, the basement was well-stocked with dried goods for the kitchen, but further away, the area became storage for the accumulated bric-a-brac of nearly two centuries, as well as furniture that was too nice to throw out but no longer usable. Every time she went down, she wondered how one family accumulated so many chairs, and why were so many of them in need of reupholstery?

She stopped once she reached the vault's door—several inches of iron and inlaid with silver and gold sigils. Unlike wards, which were static things that required recharging after creation, the living sigils that guarded the vault were composed of and fueled by dead spirits bound into never-ending service. They flashed in ever-changing patterns and made the vault one of the most magically secure areas in the world, with the exception of agencies like the Salt Mine and the Ivory Tower.

Moncrief felt the spirits writhe at her approach, but they sensed the familial blood coursing through her veins soon enough—a few of the guardians were distant ancestors of hers. She pricked her forefinger on the sharp tip of a nearby Javanese kris and traced a pattern upon the door with the small bead of blood. The crimson smear vanished into the cold smooth surface and when she removed her hand, the door clicked open.

A familiar rush ran through her as she entered and closed the door behind her. The thrill of entering a secret place was not lost on her, even after all these years, and it still felt like her parent's vault, although they had been dead for a decade. In addition to the family pieces, it held all the treasures they had collected in their brief but adventuresome lives. She still felt special for being allowed inside.

The vault was a two-story construction formed from unmortered granite waterproofed by layers of Cocciopesto plaster. The first rooms were dedicated to textiles, most of which were specific outfits for various esoteric needs, from metal-free attire for fae to special ensembles for ritual magic. The second floor contained the family occult library, several enchanted cabinets securely holding dozens of magical items, as well as the family armory—a doubly protected room the size of a spacious walk-in closet.

Moncrief retrieved the hellhound-hide book from the library that enumerated the vault's holdings. There were few magical items on the first level and the titled spines in the library made quick work, but the cabinets were not so obliging. It had been a long time since she had done an inventory of her family's cache, and she had to decipher the scrawl of each entry, written in the hand and blood of the Moncrief that had entered the item into the vault.

Things went faster with the more recent acquisitions—the Egyptian items her maternal grandparents had found, the haul from the Indian subcontinent from her paternal grandfather, and South and Central American treasures from her parents. She had just checked off the jade plaque from Chichén Itzá when she found a misplaced item—a bone needle from Sibudu Cave resting on the velvet next to the engraved stone.

"What are you doing in the Americas?" she precociously asked it. She put aside her inventory book, opened the cabinet, and gently withdrew the needle. It looked much younger than its forty thousand years, and its value went well beyond the archeological. It was one of the earliest man-made magic items.

When creatures crossed realms, they created ripples in the fabric of mortal reality, disturbances that could be seen by a practitioner through the eye of the needle. Such ripples were generally harmless, and the list of things that caused such waves was long and varied—ghosts manifesting, vampires in mist form, a person under invisibility magic, crossing into the Magh Meall, summoning a creature, planar travel, astral projection, etc. However, should an area of space-time be compromised by frequent, repeated activity or overwhelmed by summoning too powerful a fiend for the circle that was made, it was possible to tear the fabric of reality with pandemonium commensurate to the size of the rip. While the eye of the bone needle could help identify weak areas, its real utility was its ability to *repair* tears by using the blood of the wielder as thread. One could even bolster reality before a big summoning, like a tailor would reinforce a seam.

Moncrief started to walk it back to the other African items, but it occurred to her that it could be useful. Leader had said that if the master of Mau was not a practitioner, no signature would be found by salt casting, but if they saw disturbances through the eye of the bone needle, it would let them know something magical happened there—the ripples remained for some time after their causal event. If wouldn't be proof positive that it was Mau, but considering the circumstances, highly suggestive.

She retrieved the lead-lined wooden matchbox that rested nearby in the display cabinet. She wrapped the Sibudu needle in soft velvet and tucked it inside with a shake to make sure there was no rattle. Then she slipped the matchbox into her front pocket and methodically worked through the rest of the cabinets and armory. She breathed a sigh of relief when every item was present and accounted for, and her stomach grumbled for sustenance.

Moncrief returned the inventory book to its place in the library and was about to exit the vault when she remembered the one item her family had that wasn't on any list. Something they *shouldn't* have had: Mictēcacihuātl's Tongue. She steeled herself and turned back.

Mictēcacihuātl's Tongue was a foot-long obsidian dagger with two slabs of ahuehuete wood bound by human sinew for a handle. The blade was the crystallized tongue of the goddess Mictēcacihuātl—the only part of her body that remained in the mortal realm after she was killed in the seventeenth century. The Moncrief family had kept the dagger in a series of warded boxes in a secret room in the armory for the past hundred and twenty years.

On her sixteenth birthday, her parents had shown her the dagger. She remembered her father demonstrating how to open the secret room and how she'd marveled at all the sigils that specifically warded it: Mictēcacihuātl's Tongue was the only thing stored in there. He'd opened box after box and donned a pair of chainmail gloves before finally unearthing it from the salt it rested within. The dagger seemed to throb and pulse like a living thing in her father's large hands, and the light dimmed when its shiny black edge finally cleared all of the white salt. She still remembered his words: "Never touch this, Alicia. Its edge kills anything it cuts, and it can cut through anything that was once alive. It annihilates the soul of those it kills—erases it completely."

"It is never to be used or even see the light of day," her mother had stated emphatically. "No good can come from such evil."

She'd leaned away from the blade as her caution overcame her curiosity. "Then why don't you destroy it?"

"It can't be destroyed. It has already been destroyed," her mother had replied while her father sunk the dagger back into the salt and the brightness of the light returned. "It both exists and doesn't. It is the death of death, beyond the concept of being. Since it cannot be unmade, we keep it hidden away."

"And now, you are responsible for it, as we are," her father had said solemnly as he put the nestled warded boxes back in place and closed the secret door. "You are a Moncrief, and that comes with more than just money and parties. Do you understand?"

At the time, she'd answered as she was expected to—a sober yes—and she now felt the full weight of that duty as she flicked on the lights in the armory. The secret door clicked open as she turned one of the electric sconces on the wall and it glided silently on a hinged pin, revealing the mess behind it—the boxes were shattered, the salt spread thinly everywhere, and the two chainmail gloves tossed in the corner.

"Shit," she cursed forcefully as she removed the Sibudu needle from its box and held it up to her eye. The air behind the secret wall shimmered and rippled.

"Shit, shit, shit."

Chapter Thirteen

Baltimore, Maryland, USA
28th of October, 2:55 p.m. (GMT-4)

Moncrief mindlessly bit into an egg and cress sandwich as both her and Buchholz's phones buzzed yet again. The message group had blown up once she released the text that Mau's new master was in possession of Mictēcacihuātl's Tongue. In other circumstances, she would have handled it more discreetly, but if there was a chance that any of the other agents might cross its path, forewarned was forearmed.

They all knew crazy powerful things existed, but that didn't help absorb the shock of its existence and theft from the Moncriefs, one of the old magical families. They were as close to arcane royalty as any of the agents had encountered, and the report of the dagger's theft brought home the peril of having Mau away from Hor-Nebwy. The mummy kept her as a companion and only used her powers to retrieve the corpses and possessions of those he entombed. Clearly, her new master had other plans—a thief doesn't steal a weapon like Mictēcacihuātl's Tongue without intending to become a murderer.

The threat was dire enough for Leader to relax the standard

protocol from "wait until fired upon to return fire" to "do what you have to do to keep yourself safe," which was only one step away from "shoot first and ask questions later." The hardworking analysts of the Salt Mine were diving into recent murders to see if they could find a connection to any of the thefts, but it was unlikely Mictēcacihuātl's Tongue had struck yet—it left a very distinct corpse that would have appeared on the daily radar of unusual death reports.

Moncrief wallowed in her failure. Gerard tried to coax her out of her gloom by having the chef make her favorites, but all food tasted bland in her defeat. Buchholz had never seen her in such a state. Moncrief had always been the essence of wit and charm, with an intelligent spark behind her twinkling baby blues and dimples. Clover had bailed him out on more than one occasion, and the oppressive silence in the breakfast room was more than he could bear.

Even though it was well outside of his wheelhouse, he tried his best to cheer her up. "So," he started benignly, "what other contraband do you have squirreled away in this mansion? Any chance you have Mjölnir? I've always wanted to see if I was worthy…" Moncrief rolled her eyes and piled clotted cream and jam on a scone, refusing the take his bait. "It doesn't have to be magical. How about a nuke? Got any A-bombs hanging around?"

"That's not funny, Hobgoblin. I fucked up. Big time," she mumbled before taking a bite.

"Leader will get over it. She's a pragmatist and she needs you. Who else is going to fly in and save the day in Prada?" he replied breezily. "I mean, when you think about it, she should be thanking you. How many people *haven't* been killed by the dagger since it's been in your family's care?"

Moncrief shook her head dismissively. "I'm not worried about Leader," she corrected him. "I'm talking about my parents. I had one job—make sure the soul-rendering dagger doesn't get out. Somewhere between jetting around the world at the drop of a hat and pretending to be a spy, I lost sight of that," she said with bitter resignation that could not be offset by the sweet strawberry jam.

He dropped his affected levity and became very real. "Alicia, there is no way anyone could have stopped Mau from getting that dagger."

"I just don't understand how they knew where it was," she angrily rebutted. "It's been a well-guarded secret for generations and there is no way someone scried into my vault."

Buchholz knew Moncrief was way more knowledgeable about the esoteric arts than he, but he did know about picking himself up after royally screwing the pooch. "That's one of the things we're going to figure out once we catch this thief. In the meantime, I need you to pull it together and do what you do best."

"And what's that?" she asked facetiously.

"Find your angle and turn the tide in our favor. You're our

Clover," he said gently before retreating from such tenderness. "And I know for a fact, nobody messes with Alicia Elspeth Hovdenak Moncrief and gets away with it."

The smallest of smiles manifested on her face. She couldn't get a good saltcasting in the vault with all the interference of the living sigils, but now there was little doubt in her mind that Mau's thief was a magician. She still had a chance to recover Mictēcacihuātl's Tongue before it annihilated anyone, and she knew what she needed to do.

She summoned her faithful butler to the breakfast room, and recovered her commanding demeanor. "Gerard, please get Barbara Hollister on the phone and make arrangements to fly out to Cape Cod as soon as possible."

"Yes, Miss," Gerard replied.

"Oh, and can you bring more of these?" She motioned to the salmon mousse sandwiches. Suddenly, she was quite hungry.

"Of course, Miss." The butler bowed his head and kept his smile to himself until he'd cleared the threshold.

"Who is Barbara Hollister?" Buchholz asked.

"A close family friend who will welcome a last-minute visit from me and give Nathan Bauer access to the site of a robbery," she alluded to his alias in private securities with Fulcrum's Daniel Westwood.

Buchholz shifted his bearing as he dropped into character. "I guess I only have one last question," he said once he'd rediscovered Bauer's speaking cadence. Her mouth was full, but she motioned for him to proceed. He narrowed his eyes and leaned in, all serious. "You got a dragonflame sword?" He reached for another cucumber sandwich without breaking character.

"If I did, I know what I'd sheath it in," she said, reaching over the table to poke against his chest.

*****

"Alicia!" sang Barbara Hollister, the lady of Chatham House, as she greeted Moncrief with a dainty embrace and two air kisses on alternating cheeks. "So nice to see you again, my dear."

"It's good to see you too, Auntie," she answered in kind. Hollister wasn't technically related to Moncrief, but she called all her parents' close friends the familial honorific of aunt or uncle. "You look well."

"Oh, this old thing." Hollister waved dismissively at the dress she had picked out for dinner once she'd received Moncrief's call. "I hope you're hungry. I've had Emile whip up something scrumptious for dinner." Her attention wandered to the tall, handsome man that followed Moncrief into the room. The statuesque woman sized him up in the blink of an eye. "And this must be your security man?"

"Nathan Bauer at your service, ma'am," Buchholz

introduced himself with a curt bob of the head and a polite handshake.

"Apparently, there have been a spate of recent art thefts, and it appears I am its latest victim," Moncrief declared melodramatically.

"No! Which one?" Hollister was aghast.

"One the lesser Albert Oehlen's from Terra House," Moncrief put her auntie's mind to rest—it was barely worth a hundred thousand dollars, but it was the principle of the thing. "Bauer seems to think it wasn't an isolated incident and asked if any of my friends had also had pieces stolen recently, and of course, your Fontana came to mind."

Hollister couldn't remember telling Alicia about the theft, but it had been a while back—maybe ten months ago? "That was so long ago, I'm not sure I could be much help."

Moncrief smiled and spoke in code, "Auntie, Bauer provides tailored security for families requiring special consideration."

Hollister's round face lit up with comprehension—he was a practitioner! "Well, why didn't you say so? The police have been useless in recovering it, and to add insult to injury, the claim was in review when the insurance company went out of business. I'll be lucky to receive cents on the dollar once the case gets out of court," she lamented, but quickly recovered her sense of decorum. "Not that it's about the money. It's the art that's important."

"Compensation does help in the face of a loss, even if it

pales in comparison to the sentimental value," Moncrief added.

"Well said, Alicia," Hollister heartily agreed.

"If I could just see the location of the theft, that would be of great help," Bauer explained.

"Is that all?" Hollister said in disbelief. She was from a magical family but was not blessed with the touch. "Follow me," she instructed as she led them through the house and into her deceased husband's office. It was still as it was when he passed away three years ago, down to the battered brass ashtray he'd used for cigars. While he was alive, she'd vociferously been against them—a filthy habit!—but after his death, the thought of getting rid of his ashtray was too much to bear.

The walls were lined with paintings that Buchholz only recognized because Moncrief had told him what he'd find on the flight over. His cover didn't require much, but he needed at least a *little* knowledge of the subject matter. The bright white spot stood out starkly against the smoke-stained sections of walls unprotected by frames. "This is where it used to hang?" he asked.

Hollister nodded. "*Il buco dell'uovo* was one of his first works, hinting at what he'd eventually refine into his complete conception of Spatialism. It was my late husband's centerpiece."

That's a long-winded way of saying slashed monochrome canvases, Buchholz thought to himself, but he kept his cover intact. "Fontana is a bit of a departure from the rest of your late husband's collection," he tactfully stated and gestured to the landscapes and rural scenes.

"He enjoyed the dichotomy between the bucolic and the starkness of the Fontana," she stated with authority and a queer smile broke her otherwise inscrutable mien. "Then again, my late husband was a bit of a strange egg himself. He did have his opinions…"

Buchholz did a quick sweep of the room and found no cameras. "If you ladies would give me a few minutes of privacy, I'll start my investigation."

"He has proprietary methods—trade secrets and all that," Moncrief said in a cheerful but patronizing tone. She held out her arm and suggested to Hollister, "Perhaps an aperitif?"

"I shan't be more than ten minutes," Buchholz assured Hollister. "Then, I can leave you ladies to your visit." He watched Hollister's esteem of him rise, and he wasn't sure if it was because he'd said "shan't" like it was something normal people said, or if it was that he had the good manners to know he wasn't invited to dinner without her having to say as such.

"We'll be in the drawing room when you're finished," Hollister told him as they left.

He waited until he was certain they had cleared the hallway and wouldn't return before pulling out the Sibudu needle from his inner pocket. He held it to his eye and looked at the blank patch of wall—it rippled like asphalt on a hot day.

He carefully tucked the needle away—Moncrief had been very explicit at what she would do to him if it were damaged in his care—and took out his saltcaster. It took half a minute for the blown grains to shift into a pattern, and he reflexively muttered, "*Ich habe Schwein gehabt*," under his breath as he snapped a photo of the signature.

Buchholz brushed the salt away with his shoes and took additional pictures of the room and surrounding paintings—it would save him a trip if he wanted the information at a later date. He sent off a quick message with the magical signature attached. If it got a hit in the Salt Mine's database, they were one step closer to hunting down Hor-Nebwy's—and Moncrief's—thief.

He put Bauer back on before exiting the office and winding his way to the drawing room. Moncrief and Hollister were in mid-giggle when he entered the room. "Did you get everything you need?" Moncrief inquired with all lightness in her voice and manner, but Buchholz understood the undertone of the question.

"I believe so," he answered neutrally before turning to the lady of the house. "Thank you for your help, Mrs. Hollister. I'll do my best to recover your painting while in pursuit of Ms. Moncrief's property."

Hollister looked up from her drink and gave him a nod. "That would be lovely."

Moncrief reached into her purse and handed the rental's keys to Buchholz. "If you'd find your way out, I'm sure Auntie will have her driver drop me off after dinner."

"Quite right! Now, did you hear about the trouble that Mrs. Nelson got into?"

Chapter Fourteen

Buchholz checked his phone as the latest texts came through. So far, the locations of seven thefts had been scouted between the agents, and four of them bore the same magical signature as the one from Chatham House—Los Angeles, Dallas, Chicago, and Pensacola. All the other sites were absent of magical traces.

Sometime around midnight, the Salt Mine had found a match in the system to Christopher Davis Hughes, white male, age forty-nine. He was a widower with no children, with two New York residences: a flat in Manhattan and a home in Kings Point. He had a Masters in Mechanical Engineering from Stanford and a PhD in Electrical Engineering from MIT, and was a co-founder of Directed Robotics. The company produced cutting-edge semi-autonomous robots for warehouse inventory management and had recently won a government contract for a compact exploratory NASA planetary rover design. About a year ago, he'd sold his shares and left the company, citing personal reasons.

After that, the pieces started falling together, starting with how Hughes took Mau in the first place: robotics. Buchholz and Moncrief had hashed out a working theory while the G650 was being prepared for takeoff. Hor-Nebwy didn't have sight in the traditional sense, and couldn't even see the track marks in the sand until he had jumped into Buchholz's body and looked through his mortal eyes. He clearly saw objects, like sand and clothing, and he didn't have any problems seeing living things, like humans. He definitely picked up magic—Buchholz could still remember the boney finger hitting his chest where his fish amulet now hung—which would explain the inclusion of elementals and golems among his extensive wards.

But robots were a completely different beast, and it wasn't hard to imagine that Hor-Nebwy was behind the times on technology. How could the mummy include them on his non-visual radar if he didn't know they existed? They had no implicit magic, soul, or will, so his other parameters wouldn't have spotted it. As far out as it sounded, it made as much sense as a five thousand year old mummy with a cat who can walk through walls. Buchholz relished the thought that a robot was the Achilles's Heel of a being as powerful as Hor-Nebwy. It seemed so apropos.

Reviewing Hughes's financial assets made monetary gain an unlikely motive, but when the Salt Mine dug deeper into his personal life, they found an unexpected connection: Chesapeake Group, an insurance company that specialized in insuring art, that happened to be the insurer of Barbara Hollister's policy on the Fontana. It was also the same company that was under investigation three years ago when a whistleblower stepped forward about the insurance fraud ring that was being run from the top down. That whistleblower was none other than Jessica Hughes.

According to her deposition, Chesapeake Group would issue policies on moderately priced pieces of art owned by private collectors and make duplicates based on the complex visual assessments performed during the insuring period. The pieces would then be stolen and the duplicates sold as the purloined originals in four different markets: North America, China, South Asia, and either Africa or South America. Once sold, the originals would be "recovered" and the company would recoup any insurance payments that had been made to the original policyholder.

The case was ultimately dropped when the prosecution's key witness was found dead and naked, with a belt around her neck in a hotel room two weeks before her day in court. Jessica's death was ruled accidental death by misadventure despite her husband's insistence that it was foul play. Chesapeake Group carried on for a few years, but had eventually declared bankruptcy six months ago after a spate of thefts had drained their coffers. The robberies didn't garner as much press as the bankruptcy itself, since museums and institutions were spared.

The real lynch pin was when the Salt Mine found deaths with ties to the now-bankrupt Chesapeake Group. Former

CEO Leonard Worthy died of a massive heart attack three months ago while golfing in the United Arab Emirates, and former CFO Preston Cavendish was found dead in his vacation home in the Bahamas one week ago. Moncrief breathed a sigh of relief, as the coroner's report was not consistent with Mictēcacihuātl's Tongue—his heart was still in his chest. The Mine believed that Hughes had transitioned from financial avenger to physical avenger once he realized that the destroyed Chesapeake Group had corporately shielded the decision makers from the real consequences for their actions.

The twin Rolls-Royce turbofans purred at cruising altitude, pushing Moncrief's sleek plane toward New York. Buchholz had just finished breakfast and was washing down his coffee with a screwdriver—it was his favorite utilization of orange juice and as far as he was concerned, it was never too early for a drink. There were still a lot of unanswered questions that rattled Moncrief to her core. How did Hughes know about the Valley of the Magi, and where to find Mau? How did he work out Hor-Nebwy's blind spot? How does one operate a robot through a pocket dimension? Where do the thefts and the murders intersect? Assuming that Hughes was going after the people he felt were responsible for his wife's death, why steal Mictēcacihuātl's Tongue and not use it on the CFO? If he stole it after the CFO's death, why now? What had changed?

Buchholz politely listened to her conjectures, but he wasn't overly bothered by how much he didn't know. Although he'd been trained in investigation after joining the Mine, he was a fixer at heart and had been sent into plenty of situations with less information. He would do just enough investigation to hunt down the threat and finish the job. He had a bead on his target now, which was more than he had twelve hours ago. Hughes was a man looking for revenge. Vengeance was personal and messy, and constituted a logic of its own the longer one stewed in it. Personally, he had no stake with Hughes looking for justice, but it had become his business once he had stolen Hor-Nebwy's cat and Moncrief's dagger.

"Hobgoblin, are you paying attention?" Moncrief yelled and waved her hand in front of his blank face.

Buchholz stopped messing with his phone and looked up. "Sorry, I didn't catch that last bit," he sheepishly admitted.

"I asked which location you are scouting first," she repeated herself.

"I'll probably go with the Kings Point address. It's closest to his prior workplace, and everyone hates commuting. Plus, I figure you need space to build a robot to infiltrate the Valley of the Magi. Would you do your plotting in a tiny Manhattan apartment?"

"Depends on if it's above 96th street," she quipped.

"Snob," he chided her.

She took it in stride as she finished her coffee. "I'm going to be in town taking care of business, but it's nothing that can't be canceled if you need backup."

They had both thought it best to part ways after landing to keep Moncrief's cover, especially in New York where she could easily run into someone she knew. Despite that, she didn't like sending Hobgoblin alone against someone in possession of Mictēcacihuātl's Tongue.

"I'll be fine, Mom," he assured her. "I promise not to touch the pointy end of the soul-rendering dagger."

Chapter Fifteen

Kings Point, New York, USA
29th of October, 11:10 a.m. (GMT-4)

Buchholz parked his rented Volkswagen Jetta along one of the roads winding through Kings Point Park. He scorned the metallic silk blue car as it lurched when he pulled on the parking brake. It moved like a slug with a broken back, but they didn't have anything better at the sorry excuse of a rental car agency at the dinky regional airport where they'd landed. Moncrief, on the other hand, had a limo waiting for her.

He reviewed the satellite images one more time, orienting boots on the ground to the maps on the screen. Hughes's house faced east onto Manhasset Bay, and it was an older house, which meant it was relatively modest compared to many of the neighboring estates—only 4,500 square feet with pool, tennis court, and dock. Buchholz never understood the obsession rich people had with tennis, but the bird's eye view of the neighborhood revealed a slew of courts.

The Hughes's plot had some acreage, and the house sat nestled in the middle of the lot with plenty of trees and foliage for privacy, both from the road and his neighbors. He zoomed in and pathed various exit strategies for the possible scenarios of how this could go down. If this were one of his typical assignments, he would watch the place, rig it, and blow it up once he knew Hughes was inside, but this mission required finesse. He was pretty sure Mictēcacihuātl's Tongue would survive the blast, but a five-thousand-year-old mummified cat? Magical or not, mummies don't like fire.

As he committed the landscape to memory, he got a new message from the Mine—*Confirmed death in West Bay Cayman Islands via Mictēcacihuātl's Tongue. Estimated time of death evening of Oct. 27th. Victim Jerry Gailwraith, retired COO of Chesapeake Group*. He recognized the name from the previous files; Gailwraith was the sitting COO during Jessica Hughes's tenure at the insurance company. Knowing the analysts, they were already making a list of former executives and their locations as potential subsequent targets.

The pictures that accompanied the text were certainly worth a thousand words: a body missing its heart with a head covered in so much blood, it looked like it had been explosively painted red. The pulled-back shots showed the distinct spatter with chucks and gore; upon the smallest cut from the dagger, the victim's heart punched out of its chest, hovered over its head, and exploded. Assuming the pictures weren't staged, Mictēcacihuātl's Tongue had claimed its first victim in over a century.

He'd decided on a direct approach around noon. Most of Hughes's neighbors would be at work and those who stayed home might be out for lunch. Hughes didn't have a criminal record, except for a couple of speeding and parking tickets, and he wouldn't expect a heavy like Buchholz to pull up to the house and knock on the front door. There was nothing to indicate that he was the paranoid type with lots of security against a covert entry.

He put his phone away and drove to Hughes's house. It was a Dutch Colonial that had lost some of its architectural purity over the past half century, but it was far from gauche. He pulled into the round driveway and parked next to the house, just to the side of the three-car garage. Dressed in business casual attire instead of a suit, he put on character glasses with non-prescription lenses. Then, he plastered on a dispirited face, rolled his shoulders forward, and exited the economic compact car. He held the clipboard close to his body, ensuring that the blank piece of paper fastened to the board wasn't easily visible. No one liked the guy soliciting for a new utilities service provider, but no one feared opening the door to him, either. It wasn't much of a disguise, but in Buchholz's opinion, there was a lot a good agent could do with body language and facial expressions—he had already lost a few inches and gained a few pounds just from slouching and poking out his normally absent gut.

As he waited, he spooled out his will—*was mich nicht umbringt, macht mich stärker*—to check on what kinds of wards Hughes had active. He felt the presence of the three that were pretty standard among practitioners of any skill—fiends, fae, scrying—but they seemed weak, more in line with an initiate caster. However, Christopher Hughes was no beginner; he'd been registered with the Salt Mine for decades.

He mulled this incongruity while he waited, and when there was no answer, Buchholz rang again. This time, his right hand hung to his side, close to his Walther CCP. *Maybe he did spend more time at the Manhattan property?* he thought when he didn't sense any movement or sound from within.

Buchholz pantomimed defeat and returned to his car, waiting to see if that stirred some life from within—pretending not to be home in the face of an unwanted visitor wasn't just a sitcom trope—but all was still. He saw no cameras on the premises and decided to take advantage of the empty house. He liberated his tools from his luggage and made quick work of the front door lock with his picks. Gun out, he quickly opened the door, silently slid into the house, and closed it behind him.

The marble-tiled entryway was stained with dried blood, now reddish-brown in an irregular oblong shape. There was a set of bloody handprints beside it, as well as footprints that led deeper into the house, staining the marble and white carpet behind the hall. *Yet another reason white carpet is a terrible design choice*, he impulsively infused humor to counteract the sinking feeling in the pit of his stomach. He'd seen enough professional hits to know the story the scene told. While it was possible that Hughes took a bullet and survived, when coupled with the weakening wards it was much more likely that he was now deceased. The *ambulatory* kind.

Buchholz quietly unpocketed his saltcaster and gave it a blow over the bloody scene. He kept his weapon up—thankfully loaded with banishing bullets—while he waited for the salt to work itself out. It was a simple diagnostic test that would tell Buchholz what he was dealing with. If the magical signature was the same, Hughes was alive and possibly injured—there was always the chance the blood wasn't his. If it was entirely different, there was a second practitioner in the picture... perhaps Hughes had a partner they hadn't uncovered? If it was basically Hughes's signature with slight modifications, he was undead.

Undead came in many different varieties, and if an adept reader of the saltcaster knew the practitioner's signature in life, they could identify what type of undead the magician had become based on how it had been changed. The white grains started to shake and move against the dark stain. *Please be a zombie, or a draugr*, Buchholz prayed to whatever was listening. *Be something slow, preferably stupid and slow. Be something easy to put down.*

He kept his eyes and Walther focused down the hall until he saw the movement stop in his peripheral vision. A quick glance revealed crooked additions and newly conjoined bits meaning only one thing—Christopher Hughes was a revenant, a soul with unfinished business. Revenants were nasty. Buchholz thought of them as the special forces of the non-immortal undead—fast, strong, intelligent, and relentless, with the added bonus of being unencumbered by the physical demands of a living body.

Revenants pretty much looked like they did during life, except their irises were a pinkish-violet, like albinos, and they had an affinity to where they were formed. If Hughes was here, he would know that Buchholz had entered and he would be waiting somewhere within. He'd use his knowledge of the house to his advantage. Buchholz didn't like those odds and decided on the only reasonable course of action—he waited in the entryway, gun ready. As long as he didn't move or make a sound, he would eventually draw out the revenant from its hiding place and into the line of fire. If Buchholz was wrong and Hughes wasn't here, he would only waste some time before investigating the house. He'd have ample warning should Hughes return.

There were only two ways into the hall: the main living room, with the aforementioned white carpet, and an opening to what looked like the kitchen on the left. After five tense minutes, he heard a creak in the ceiling above him. It was the slightest thing, something that could easily have been missed by the unwary. Buchholz shifted his grip on his gun and maintained a chest-high bead on the right—the side where the stairs would most likely be given the footprint of the house.

Come on, come on, he thought nervously, just waiting for

Hughes to round the corner. Buchholz heard another subtle noise and forced himself to be patient. When Hughes came for him, he would have to clear the wall first and Buchholz wanted to wait until he could see the outline of Hughes's head before shooting him center mass. Finally, a form appeared and Buchholz fired. It was immediately followed by a scream and a thud as his target fell to the floor. Buchholz smiled. The best part of banishment bullets was that it didn't have to be a stellar shot for the magic to take; he just had to hit.

There was no blood nor splatter coming from the body. Revenants didn't need any, and Hughes had already bled out in the entryway so there was no additional blood hanging around. Buchholz circled the body and kicked out his foot, making contact with the top of the corpse's head to make sure the animating spirit of the revenant no long occupied the body. He shot another round into its head to make *absolutely* sure, then took several steps back and holstered his Walther, contemplating his next move.

The banishment bullet was a stopgap measure because revenants couldn't really be killed. Fire, dismemberment, banishment bullets: nothing permanently got rid of them. No matter what happened to the body, the spirit would reform to continue its rampage. How long it took to return to a corporal state varied, but twenty-four hours was the Salt Mine's informational standard, give or take a few hours.

The only way to permanently decommission a revenant

was to put its spirit at rest, and that required the death of all those it was after or a complicated and deeply emotional magical ritual. He had a basic understanding of how to do the ritual, but he wasn't sure he could pull it off. The practitioner had to empathize with the revenant and through the sharing of emotions, cleanse them. Buchholz had a lot of strong points, but for all his many virtues, empathy wasn't one of them. He stared at what was left of Hughes and remembered Deacon's words when he'd taught him the ritual: "It's not the anger you have to understand or the thirst for vengeance. You gotta find the pain behind it all: the horror of an irrevocable loss. You gotta feel it and you gotta move through it."

The more he thought about it, the more he realized he wasn't up to the task. It would take time to call for backup, but it was worth the wait to know it was done properly…and it wasn't like Hughes was going anywhere. He pulled out his phone and was scrolling his contact list to find Deacon when a thought occurred to him. Mictēcacihuātl's Tongue permanently destroyed anything that had once lived, and it was lying right there. All he had to do was stab the bastard and let the dagger do its thing. There wouldn't even be a messy blood spatter because Hughes's ticker was tapped out.

Buchholz shrugged. *It's worth a shot.* He tucked his phone away and approached the knife from the handle side. It seemed to throw shade well beyond its contours on the white carpet. He carefully grabbed a hold of the wooden handle with his left hand and immediately regretted his decision. The knife writhed and twisted, as if it were a living thing. It felt like holding the head of a deadly snake that wanted nothing more than to bite its handler.

His lizard brain wanted to throw it away, but he held fast. There was no telling what Mictēcacihuātl's Tongue would do once it was out of his grasp, and he didn't relish the idea of it turning like a boomerang to seek his flesh. "Well, this wasn't one of your better ideas," he said aloud, holding the knife at arm's length. He didn't want to let go of it, but he also didn't want to keep holding it.

Wer A sagt, muss auch B sagen, he thought as he brought the tip of the knife against the bloodless flesh of the corpse. The tip popped the skin like an overripe grape, and the violet eyes of Christopher Hughes opened abruptly. He thrashed at Buchholz and landed a solid hit, sending the agent flying across the room. Buchholz kept his focus on holding Mictēcacihuātl's Tongue as far from his body as he could. Unable to brace for impact without bringing the dagger closer, he crashed hard against the back of the sofa, nearly losing his wind.

The momentum turned the sofa over on him like the lid of a coffin, and he'd barely gotten his Walther CCP out of its holster when the revenant threw off the couch. Buchholz put another banishing bullet into Hughes, this time his leg; he dropped like a marionette with cut strings.

"Goddamn, you are strong and fast," he grumbled at the

empty shell of a body. Buchholz winced as he stood and assessed the damage. His shoulder was going to be bruised to hell, but he was thankful he didn't break a rib in the process. He spitefully put another bullet in the corpse and called Moncrief. The black knife fought him every step of the way, and he thanked the fates that he hadn't picked up the dagger with his right hand. He'd be dead if had—he wouldn't have had time to pull his gun out of its holster with his left hand.

"This is Alicia," she answered bubbly. The indistinct babble of conversation and the clicking of utensils on plates told him she was having lunch somewhere.

"I need the containment box," he said without introduction.

"You found it?" The relief in her voice was palpable. She quickly followed up with, "You okay?"

"I'm fine, just a little beat up. Hughes is a revenant, but temporarily down for the count. I'm going to call in Deacon for the cleansing," he quickly got her up to speed.

"You're not going to do it?" she asked obliquely.

"The bastard tried to kill me twice, and I've put four banishment bullets in him. I seriously doubt he's going to listen to me when I tell him to go into the light," he said sarcastically. "Oh, and that dagger of yours…the one that's supposed to be the 'death of death' and all that shit? Well, it doesn't kill revenants; it brings them back."

"You picked it up!" she yelled a whisper over the line.

He was thankful she was in a public place and couldn't

unleash her unabridged opinion. He already knew the litany of stupid things he'd done before thinking them all the way through. "Alicia, you can yell at me all you want once it's safely contained. Just bring the box, quick."

She heard something tired and desperate in his voice and went into action. "Hold tight. I'll be there in less than an hour."

It was a long forty-three minutes before Moncrief showed up, and Buchholz didn't want to know how many moving violations her driver must have committed to make that sort of time from wherever she'd been to Kings Point. She cleared the room before lowering her gun. "You are a real dumbass," she declared as she put her gun away in her pale pink satin Dolce & Gabbana bag.

"So I've been told," he agreed with her; he was too tired to fight.

Moncrief brought in a petite box that was indistinguishable from a large makeup kit on the outside. Once she opened it, the glowing sigils inside shined and lit up the salt within. She donned the chainmail gloves brought from her vault and carefully took possession of Mictēcacihuātl's Tongue. Buchholz breathed freely for the first time since he had touched the dagger as she buried it into the salt and secured the lid.

She took a seat on the ground next to him with the containment box and Hughes in clear sight. She straightened her skirt so it wouldn't wrinkle. "Deacon coming?" she asked.

"On his way, but he's flying in from Ohio," he answered.

"You hungry? I can bring us some food if you are okay to babysit Hughes for a bit," she offered.

"Didn't you just come from a restaurant?" he snidely remarked.

Without breaking character, she replied, "Yes, but my lunch was rudely interrupted."

Chapter Sixteen

The cold white-blue headlights of Clarence Morris's rental cut through the night, sending shadows through the windows of the Hughes residence as he pulled through the circular drive. Buchholz eased the curtain a measure and caught sight of Morris's husky form in his camel-hair overcoat climbing out of the driver seat. "Deacon's here," he announced to Moncrief.

"Finally," she sighed, standing up and stretching. She had changed out of her designer suit and into her covert black wear, but she kept the containment box and her gun close by. Normally, they wouldn't have to worry about the spirit returning to the body for a while, but neither of them knew what exposure to Mictēcacihuātl's Tongue would do to the recovery time, if anything at all. They took turns watching the body at first, but as the hours passed, they felt it was safer for both of them to keep watch until Morris had arrived.

They had holed up in an upper-story bedroom with the deceased Mr. Hughes on the bed, tightly trussed with a ragtag collection of ropes and chains cobbled from what was found in the garage. It wouldn't hold once the revenant awoke, but it would slow it down long enough for them to shoot him again. Revenants could not be long contained by physical restraints; they would eventually gain enough strength to break themselves free. When he was still training with Morris, Buchholz had seen a revenant's unstoppable strength in action—one had ripped through the vault-like door of a panic room.

"You want to bring him up while I keep eyes on Mr. Chumbawamba here?" Buchholz alluded to Hughes. Moncrief nodded and switched on the light before descending, leaving the bedroom door open behind her.

The lyrical chime of the doorbell sounded, and Buchholz heard the muffled sounds of their greeting—Morris's deep rumble and Moncrief's high-pitched laugh.

"Hobgoblin! What foolishness have you gotten yourself into now? It's a good thing you called in the *real* talent," Morris shouted as he climbed the stairs. His heavy steps clomped on the steps with purpose.

"The revenant requested a down-and-out pensioner before I knocked him out of the body, and I immediately thought of you," Buchholz greeted his former mentor with a warm clasp of the hands. He winced as Morris backed it up with a slap on the shoulder but he didn't pull away from the fatherly gesture.

Morris put down his black leather medical bag and started unbuttoning his jacket. "First, it's not pensioner, it's retiree. You're in America now. Second, I'm only fifty-seven, and I'm *still* cleaning up your shit," he responded with an exaggerated shake of his head. He turned his attention to the trundled corpse lying on the bed. "I'm assuming this is the poor sonofabitch in question?"

"None other than the late Mr. Christopher Hughes," Buchholz introduced him. "We've put what you'll need on the dressing table. We're not a hundred percent sure they're his dead wife's, but there's no evidence of a girlfriend since her passing and everything was pretty dusty."

Morris perused the collection of feminine objects on the table: brushes, clothing, jewelry, and beauty supplies. He picked up a diamond ring with an interlocking wedding band and inspected it. "This will work," he declared. He opened his bag and started setting up for the ritual, starting with a solid silver cross larger than his hand.

"If you don't need me for anything else, I've got a few places to check out," Buchholz said impatiently.

Morris inquisitively raised an eyebrow. "Kitty not at home?"

"Nope, and none of the stolen paintings, either," Buchholz confessed. He had searched the house and outbuildings after Moncrief brought lunch but came up short. He had three locations to check out, courtesy of the analysts: a warehouse in Hughes's name not far from his old office, two climate-controlled storage units Hughes had rented in one of those twenty-four-hour places, and his Manhattan apartment.

"Are all the blinds shut and curtains drawn?" Morris grilled him. "I'm going to put on one hell of a light show before it's over, and this is the kind of neighborhood where the police show up quick when called. I like you and all, but I'm not looking to get shot tonight."

"Done and done," Buchholz attested. It was one of the first things he'd checked once Moncrief arrived and there was another set of eyes to watch Hughes.

"Then get out of here, dumbass! You're upsetting Mr. Hughes." Morris smiled to let him know there were no hard feelings—this was just the opening salvo on gaining the revenant's trust. He raised his large hand and pointed to Moncrief. "You? You can stay. Everyone likes the company of a pretty lady." Moncrief gave him a mischievous grin but a demure curtsy.

"Hey, that's workplace discrimination," Buchholz decried as he grabbed his things along with Hughes's ring of keys.

"It's not discriminatory; everyone doesn't like you," Morris quipped, and Moncrief stifled a giggle—the only thing nicer than the company of a pretty lady was making one laugh.

"Call me if things go tits up and you need backup," he said, content to let Morris get the last laugh in.

Morris gave him a nonchalant wave with a matching smirk. "Boy, get moving. That cat ain't going to find itself."

Buchholz's rental was cold in the late October night and it didn't warm up until his pulled into the light industrial complex. He drove in circles until he figured out the numbering scheme. The Jetta's wheels bit into the gravel parking lot as he parked in front of Hughes's building. After a few tries, he found the right key and let himself in.

It was dark, but Buchholz managed to find the master switch with a few judicious sweeps of his flashlight. The overhead lights flickered on and illuminated the warehouse. It was an overgrown workshop, covered with materials, tools, machines, and plenty of dust. He found robots in various states of completion, from a cluster of parts to a small rover with treads that resembled the marks in the Valley of the Magi.

In the far corner behind some steel shelves, Buchholz spotted a conspicuously clean spot. It was a slate slab, the kind practitioners used to make sure the lines of their circles were fully connected. He pulled out his saltcaster and threaded out his will, looking for hidden compartments, magical items, or active spells and came up short. Whatever magic Hughes had performed here, it was done and dusted. More annoyingly, there was no trace of Mau or the paintings.

Buchholz climbed back into the car and turned the heater on full blast. The engine hadn't had time to grow cold, and it was a tolerable drive to America's Best Storage, a climate-controlled, six-story concrete affair that never closed. The lobby smelled of cardboard boxes and conspicuous consumption, and the six-foot-six bearded weirdo on the other side of the counter reeked of rum.

Buchholz gathered his will as he approached the tattooed giant. "Christopher Hughes to visit my units," he said, taking out his driver's license.

The worker groggily looked at the license and typed the name his brain had been convinced to see onto the computer in front of him.

"Welcome to America's Best Storage, Mr. Hughes," he replied by rote. "Which unit do you want to access?"

"Both," Buchholz replied curtly.

"And you have your keys?" the attendant followed the routine script.

"Sure thing," he answered, holding up Hughes's hefty keyring.

The big man shrugged. "It's all yours," he replied, typing in the final required fields before ignoring him completely.

Ah, the je ne sais quoi of night shift, Buchholz waxed poetic as he took the elevator to the top floor. The air was stale, and they were playing some pretty horrid Muzak but he counted his blessings—it wasn't Christmas music. Yet.

The units on the top floor were the largest available—twenty feet by twenty feet—and Hughes's two units were adjacent to each other. On the second try, Buchholz matched the right key to the lock and rolled up the first door. The room was filled with thin wooden crates of various sizes, but none were more than a foot thick. Some had lids but other were draped with bedsheets. He did a quick scan to confirm his suspicions when he locked eyes on Barbara Hollister's Fontana. *Il buco dell'uovo* was a canvas covered in white paint with a hole punched through it. *Egg hole, indeed*, he translated the Italian in his head. He briefly tried to think of a better way to launder money than buying ridiculously overpriced modern art, but came up short.

As tempting as rummaging through millions in art was, Buchholz locked down the unit once he saw Mau was not there. He opened the second unit on the first try; it was only half full, but sitting on one of the crates was a mummified cat.

"*Ich habe Katze gehabt*," he joked, twisting the German idiom to fit his situation. He reached for her but hesitated briefly, uncertain of how to handle such a delicate object of such importance. He pulled a bedsheet off a stack of boxes and snapped the dust off. He gently picked up the mummy—it was light, dry, and smelled less musty than he thought it would. "Hi, Mau. I'm going to take you back to Hor-Nebwy," he said aloud—it felt rude to move the cat without saying something. If Mau had heard him, she didn't deign a response.

He carefully wrapped the sheet around the mummy, both to protect it and conceal it. The guy downstairs was clearly not winning employee of the month anytime soon, but Buchholz imagined even he would find a mummified cat coming through the lobby memorable.

He fired off a quick communication to the Salt Mine. They would take care of the warehouse and missing art, but his primary objective was returning Mau. It was the middle of the night when he pulled up next to Deacon's rental car. Despite the shuttered windows, he could see the lights cycle through the colors of the rainbow through the cracks and seams. When the seventh iteration of violet rolled around, the illumination returned to normal and Buchholz knew it was safe to enter. The ritual was done, and the absence of wailing and calamity meant it had worked.

He exited the car with Mau in hand and rang the bell. After a brief wait, Moncrief opened the door. "Hobgoblin, what are you doing? Don't you have the keys?" She shooed him inside.

"Mummy recovery services," he grinned. "Anyone here order a dead cat?"

Chapter Seventeen

Valley of the Magi
Somewhere in Time

Hor-Nebwy stood in the tomb, grinding stone to stone as he gave depth to the chalked symbols he'd drawn earlier. His whole body rocked in repetitive motion as each pass slowly etched deeper into the sandstone. His shadow danced on the wall, cast by the superfluous light of the primitive clay lamp. The mummy had worked non-stop since his encounter with the Hobgoblin. He had great confidence in the Faithful One's servant and soon, Mau would be returned. It was only a matter of time before he had the prized gem of Avalon in his domain.

Hor-Nebwy held no animosity toward the island nor its keepers. He applauded their attempt at providing a final resting place for those who died with valor. Viviane and her sisters did their best, but they were fickle and their gaze inconstant. Over time, they had increasingly shifted their mortuary responsibilities to their servants as they flitted and out of worlds, to say nothing of the horror of keeping the dead in such moist conditions. No, good intentions could not compensate for their dereliction of duty. Avalon wasn't a place that would live forever and in Hor-Nebwy's thinking, it was therefore dying—entirely unfit to contain the remains of humanity's greatest warriors against evil.

He ran his fingers and sightless vision over the finished hieroglyph and found it good. For eons, he had relied solely on his arcane sight, but his time with the Hobgoblin reminded him of what mortal senses were like—so limited, yet refreshing in their naïveté. He'd cast his will into dead bodies plenty of times—it was his preferred method of communication when he had to contact someone in the mortal realm—but things looked very different through living eyes.

Hor-Nebwy moved to the next symbol and began carving out the sandstone. He wanted the tomb to be ready for Arthur when he finally arrived with Excalibur in hand, and he still had all the painting to do after this. The faint hint of a song interrupted the rhythmic rumble of his grinding. He stopped his labor but kept the stone on the wall, cocking his head for a closer listen—it was the droning chorus of the Hobgoblin. *Mau has returned! So soon!*

He contained his excitement and set down his tools. With a flick of his will, he snuffed the flame of the clay lamp. With a single step, Hor-Nebwy left the completely dark tomb and walked upon the endless sand sea surrounding the Valley of the Magi. He aligned himself precisely to the song's location and took another step. With a gesture of his hand, he opened a path into the mortal realm and stepped through.

"That is enough," he commanded the Hobgoblin. He wore the same white and red shendyt as last time, but next to the prostate man was the proud cat mummy Hor-Nebwy needed to fulfill his promise.

"Great Hor-Nebwy, I have brought that which has been taken from you," Buchholz ingratiated himself. The mummy crackled as he reached down and picked up his oldest companion. Buchholz had never heard a mummy laugh before and would gladly go the rest of his life—and afterlife—without hearing it again.

"And the thief?" he inquired.

"I assure you, Great Hor-Nebwy, that the thief was in soul-wrenching agony before he was sent to the Land of the Dead," Buchholz answered solemnly.

Hor-Nebwy heard the truth in his words and smiled. "You have done well, the Hobgoblin. Tell your master her debt has been paid." He left the cowering human and stepped back into the Valley of the Magi, Mau in hand. He tenderly looked her over; in his vision, he saw the Mau that curved around his living ankles, purring as she passed. All the parts were where they were meant to be, but he tsked at her overall state. "You have been mistreated," he said with a frown, after taking full stock of her condition. "Much too damp!"

He reached down and scooped up some sand. He focused his will and moved a nearly imperceptible amount of moisture from the small mummy into the grains in his hand. He then cast the sand in a wide arc onto the surrounding dunes. Any water within the sand dissipated as it hit the ground. Hor-Nebwy examined Mau again and grunted his pleasure.

He placed the mummy onto the dune and raised his call.

"Mau, I am in need of your service." His sepulchral voice traveled beyond the veil between the living and the dead, and he waited until the susurration of sand upon sand was broken by the crunching sound of Mau's paws exiting her mummified skin. The black cat languidly stretched and groomed herself before finally sitting on her haunches, the perfect image of the ancient Egyptian cat statue. "Meow," the cat said in a greeting of sorts.

"And to you as well, fellow ancient one," he returned her salutations. "I have made an agreement for your services, and your temporary master has requested you obey."

Feeling the veracity of his words, Mau nodded, stretched once more, and leapt into the air. She disappeared at the apex of her jump and landed in Avalon. The hair on her back immediately rose—this was a place of danger. She had little time and immediately sniffed the air, searching for the scent of her new master.

She felt a force pulling her forward but was still unable to determine the exact location of the source. She ran to the top of the nearest hill and hissed in anger—the monotony of hill after hill offended her. Everything smelled so alive and green, but underneath it all, she locked onto a scent. It was small and sad, and if scent had a color, this one would be gray.

Mau bounded toward the acrid odor, getting stronger with each mound she crested. When she found her target, it was little more than a shadow tethered to the ground by strands of ebon mist, but it persisted in pulling itself through the lush grass of Avalon. On its back lay a body wrapped in rags and more substantial than its bearer. Behind it trailed a single strap attached to a long and slim object bound in cloth. It all smelled sour, like something once human that had gone off.

The sorry state of her new master stirred something in Mau that she had not felt in five thousand years. In a blink, she grew to the size of a tiger and pinned the ebon specter to the ground with one large black paw and gave it a good lick. It was hurt and licks cured hurts. It struggled under her paw, and she remembered how her own younglings had struggled the same way. They too had resisted being cleaned, even though it was for their own good. Mau lapped, nipped, and nuzzled the crawling shadow, hoping to restore it to a travel-worthy state.

With each pass of her prickly tongue, Mau came to understand more. It had once been a he, and his soul had been burned and shredded. Avalon had stepped in and kept him from dying, but now the fibers of Avalon bound him to the place. He would die if Mau took him away, yet that was her purpose and his last command. Befuddled by the conundrum, she proceeded to do what instinct told her was right: continue grooming him.

Bit by bit, flakes of him came off on her rough tongue, and her cleaning became more vigorous as the weight of Avalon started pressing against her. Once one spot was clean, it only brought her attention to just how much the rest of him needed washing. In her zeal, another memory broke through—the birth of her litter.

Struck by inspiration, Mau turned her attention away from the crawling shadow to the ties that bound him to Avalon. She bit through a black band, licking the wounds she made by severing the cord. When it healed beneath her tongue, she moved onto the next one. She worked furiously at freeing him, as if at any moment a predator would top the nearby hill and pounce. When the last link was broken, she gripped the shadow by the scruff of his neck and vaulted into the air.

Mau landed upon a soft bed, far, far away from Avalon. She felt her arrival trigger an alarm, but she paid it no heed—nothing could bind her in the mortal realm. She fought the urge to retrigger the alarm again and again, just to let them know she didn't care.

She released her cargo from her mouth and shrank back to her preferred size. The inky haze was gone and the shadow morphed into the shape of a human, although the body he carried remained dead. David Emery Wilson was reborn in his own bed, safely behind the wards of the 500. He rolled the body of Arthur onto the floor and with it, Excalibur wrapped in tattered tunics. He reached out and petted the black cat that sat beside him on his bed. "Thank you, Mau. You may return to Hor-Nebwy with those," he said before falling into a heavy sleep with a smile on his face.

Mau circled Wilson, sniffing and tasting his new form. There was an undeniable muskiness to him, but the fetid rancidity was gone. She walked through his apartment, blinking through walls and wards with ease. She smelled something interesting and ripped open a box of crackers and ate her fill. She had never been to this place, this "Detroit" before, and she found it acceptable. Curiosity of her immediate environs sated, Mau returned to Wilson, who was still soundly sleeping. She sauntered past him a few times, flicking her tail. Eventually, she curled up and took shelter in the crook of his arm, lulled to sleep by his steady breath.

Chapter Eighteen

Detroit, Michigan, USA
31st of October, 2:45 a.m. (GMT-4)

Leader paced the perimeter of 500 10th Street, the heavily guarded residence of Fulcrum. There were no gun turrets, trenches, barricades, or barbed wire, but magically speaking, it was a verifiable fortress. When he'd gone missing, she'd kept an eye on the wards for fading—a definitive sign that he was deceased.

She didn't have much hope for his survival after she'd received his email about his bargain with Baba Yaga, and as expected, his protections did start to weaken. Were it any other of her agents, she would have simply brute-forced her way in when the wards started to go down, but Fulcrum's obsession with security was only surpassed by his ability. Who knew how many dead man's switches he'd put into his wards? Unwilling to take chances when patience would solve the problem, Leader had simply put an alarm over the building to notify her when the wards had lost all their power or of entry onto the premises. She didn't know what materials Wilson had gathered for his practice, but she'd rather keep all of it out of anyone else's hands. He was the best summoner she'd encountered in decades, and that study was the most dangerous of their arts.

When her alarm was tripped, she had first thought nothing of it—finally, Fulcrum's security was down and it was time to round up his things and put the hazardous objects away. It was only after she arrived that she'd found his wards very much intact. The 500 was occupied again by something that had only triggered her alarm. Leader bore her hawkish gray eyes on the 500, but found no new insight that had previously eluded her. The building was dark and there were no signs of life, arcane or otherwise. Her brow furrowed as she walked back to the parked SUV.

"Oh, that can't be good," Dot commented from the back seat. Chloe nudged her sister's side and waited for Leader to get inside. They waited for her to say something, but she was busy ruminating.

"Has he finally passed?" Chloe asked softly after the dome light had timed out and dimmed.

"No, the wards are still intact." Leader sighed.

"I knew it! No way Wilson would let Baba Yaga punk him. He's back, baby!" Dot declared triumphantly. "You owe me dinner, Chloe."

Leader allowed Dot to finish gloating before speaking. "David, would you scout? I hate to ask, but…" His keen eyes saw the small apologetic shrug of her shoulders despite the darkness.

"Certainly," he crisply replied and stepped out of the driver's seat. His tall, wide form strode across the street to the sidewalk that surrounded the 500. He slowly circumnavigated the building, sniffing as he went. It took a while, but his sensitive nose eventually picked something up. He jogged back to the SUV and posed a question. "Did Hobgoblin come anywhere near here during his mission?"

"He didn't report it if he did," she answered and turned to the twins. "Did he say anything to either of you?" They shook their heads no. "Why do you ask?"

"Mau's been here," he said solemnly.

"Was this before or after we gave the cat back to Hor-Nebwy?" Chloe inquired.

"My nose is good, but it can't tell time," LaSalle lamented.

"It would have to be after," Leader replied. "I put this alarm up weeks ago, and it's the same basic build as what I put on the Salt Mine to detect an unwanted visit from Mau once we found out she was stolen. At the time it was triggered, Mau was already back with Hor-Nebwy; Hobgoblin reported to me immediately after it was done." The warded blast-resistant vehicle fell silent as they pondered the significance of this find.

"What would Hor-Nebwy want from Wilson's place?" Chloe puzzled.

"Did he have us retrieve his cat so he could steal something from Wilson?" Dot huffed incredulously at the gall. "Frankly, I didn't think Wilson had anything that cool in his cache."

Leader locked eyes with LaSalle in the rearview mirror.

"Are you sure about Mau?" she asked.

"Positive," he affirmed.

Leader's phone rang in her inner pocket, and the screen lit up. "Unknown caller," she said for the benefit of the others before she answered. "Hello."

"You guys can all come in if you want," Wilson said straight away, bypassing formality. Leader looked out the window toward the 500. A light came on in one of the fourth-floor rooms, and silhouetted against it was the thin frame of a man with a bushy beard. As he waved, the black outline of a cat jumped onto the windowsill. The voice sounded right, but Leader was suspicious nonetheless. If Fulcrum had made it through the ordeal of the Russian witch, at what cost? Was he even Wilson anymore?

"You've been gone a long time," Leader replied neutrally, casting her will through the phone.

"It's a long story and I'm sure you have a lot of questions, which I will answer, but I'm famished. Once I hang up with you, I'm calling a twenty-four-hour pizza place that delivers and I can just as easily order more pizzas if you'd care to join me," he offered. "And Chloe and Dot and LaSalle, of course."

Leader pressed her will further and responded with a noncommittal, "Naturally."

"Oh, fair warning, I stink to high heaven, so better give me time to shower," he said as an aside. "Any requests?" he casually inquired. Chloe and Dot were on the edge of their seats, pantomiming all sorts of questions to Leader.

Leader wound her will around each syllable and found nothing untoward or malicious. "Let me check," she replied. She shifted the phone and addressed the occupants of the SUV. "Fulcrum wants to know what we want on our pizza."

*****

"So that's the gist of it," Wilson finished and stroked his long beard. He had every intention of shaving it, but the luxury of a longer hot shower was too good to pass up. As it was, he was still damp when the food and his guests entered through the massive jaws of his garage door. In total, he'd ordered four pizzas—two for them, one for Mau, and one for himself. He was hungry with a capital H. "And you can see my dilemma," he opened the narrative up for questions and suggestions while chewing on the last bones of his Italian sausage, bell pepper, and red onion pizza.

Leader, Chloe, Dot, and LaSalle sat on his leather sectional, soaking in details and letting them percolate. It was the first time Wilson had had people over at the 500; his living room had largely been furnished by custom—he'd bought the couches and coffee table because that's what a living room looked like. The intimate conviviality of the affair was new to him. After such an encounter, he would have expected to go through the Process and be debriefed in Leader's office. Instead, the remains of their drinks and pizza were on the table, and Mau was licking her pizza box for any lingering traces of the anchovies that were on her pie.

As fantastic as the tale was, they had all lived through crazier and had no reason to believe Wilson was lying—he'd let each of them have a go at magically probing him upon entry. He was definitely changed, but still essentially Wilson, even if some of the rough edges had been ground down. He smiled and graciously greeted them and hugged the librarians on sight. They could tell how painfully thin he was under his clothing in their collective embrace.

Wilson opened his home to them, dropping all the wards, not just to the exterior door, but also to the staircase leading to his elevated living space as well as every interior door within the public spaces of his apartment. He even dropped the wards on his kitchen cabinets while he made them a hot beverage, since he was trying to let them know he had nothing to hide. There was a depth to his account that had been lacking from all the other reports he'd given over the years. Whatever he was, he was more Wilson than any of them had ever seen.

And then there was Mau. Everyone understood the power of the pact, and the fact that Wilson was out of Avalon but the legendary cat, the body of Arthur, and Excalibur were still in his apartment was a messy quandary. That was the reason Wilson broke standard protocol and opted for an immediate briefing—Mau didn't want to go back to Hor-Nebwy.

Mau, on the other hand, saw no problems. She was fascinated by salty fish on bread and devoured it gleefully. It was nicer than crackers, although crackers weren't bad. She had much to learn about Detroit. She generally stayed close to Crawling Shadow, but she sniffed at the others for completeness. Superficially, the Faithful One reminded her the most of her old master, but when Mau looked deeper, she saw the differences and let her stay. Two Souls had scratches and pats that were almost as nice as Crawling Shadow, and the drama between them pleased Mau's nature. Ghost Walker was the only of them to look back at Mau, and the intensity of his gaze had made her leap back into Crawling Shadow's arms.

"I don't understand," Leader said when she finally broke her silence. "When you made your pact, you exerted your will in regards to transferring Mau back to Hor-Nebwy once you returned to Detroit."

"I have a theory," Chloe chimed in. "You said Mau groomed you in Avalon?" Wilson nodded. He still remembered the bristly tongue against his nebulous form. "Perhaps she swallowed some of your soul."

"Isn't that a bad thing?" Wilson hedged. "Having a bit of someone else's soul inside me was what started this fiasco."

"That was because you had your own living soul in there too," Chloe pointed out. "Mau hasn't been alive for a long time nor has she had her own free will since being mummified. Hor-nebwy created her to be a servant and companion."

"But now, Mau is her own kitty," Dot cooed, coaxing the luxurious black cat near her with a scrap of her pizza. Mau deigned to sit in Two Souls's lap while she worked on the crust.

Perplexed, Wilson asked, "So does that make me her master?"

Mau looked up and said, "Free," in a raspy voice. She didn't need to vocalize to communicate with Crawling Shadow, but she wanted the others to understand that she was her own master now. She resumed gnawing on the end of the crust while everyone digested that.

Chloe scratched behind Mau's ears and addressed Wilson. "A pact's a pact. You know what happens if you break it," she warned.

"But I haven't broken it," Wilson insisted. "I tried to send her back with Arthur and Excalibur. I've fully honored my end. I'm karmically clean."

"I don't think Hor-Nebwy will see it that way," Dot said darkly, stroking the cat's shiny coat.

Mau jumped off Dot's lap and growled. She grew to the size of a bobcat and hissed, "Not property!"

"It's all right, Mau," Wilson comforted her by putting both hands around her large head and looking into her emerald eyes. "You're not going back. We're just trying to figure out how to keep me from getting killed in the process."

"Take you away. No one catch. Too fast," Mau boasted.

"No one can catch you," he agreed, "but I'm not that quick.

I'll get caught eventually."

Mau considered his words and couldn't argue. He was slow. She shrank back to her normal size and crawled into his lap.

"What I'm saying is that I need a play and quick," Wilson said to Leader.

She nodded and addressed Mau, "How long until Hor-Nebwy thinks you've been gone too long."

The cat raised and tilted her head, considering, "Already."

"Shit," Dot cursed. "Any way to get to him first?"

"No. He never leaves his valley for more than a moment, and we don't stand a chance on his turf," Chloe answered.

"Not to mention his command of the dead," LaSalle interjected.

Wilson was touched they were preparing to go to the mattresses to save his hide, and Mau marginally lowered any disdain she had for them at first glance.

"There may be a way to resolve this without going to war," Leader pointed out. She had run through a myriad of possible solutions, but she didn't want to destroy the Valley of the Magi nor reveal her backdoor into it. With that in mind, she crafted a plan where everyone would get what they wanted, including herself. "Wilson, would it be all right to invite Hobgoblin into this?"

Wilson was startled—it was the first time she had called him anything except Fulcrum since his hire, and definitely the first time Leader asked his permission on anything. "Sure."

Leader turned to LaSalle. "David, would you call in Hobgoblin and ask him to bring his necklace."

Chapter Nineteen

Detroit, Michigan, USA
31st of October, 9:45 a.m. (GMT-4)

"What do you mean the closest dead cat's in Cleveland?" Buchholz shouted into the archaic receiver in his office.

"I'm sorry, sir, but you've caught us at a low-stock period. All of the institutions just put in their big orders for the year and it's going to be a week until we get our next restock. The preservation process takes time." The voice on the other end was apologetic, but in that sorry-not-sorry way.

"So I'm just supposed to drive three hours, each way, to get a cat for my kid to cut open?" he asked incredulously.

"I'm afraid so. Perhaps you could order online and maybe rush a delivery?" she suggested.

"No, just give me the address," he mumbled, and jotted it down on a notepad.

"Is there anything else I can do for you today, sir?" she asked in a chipper tone.

"No, you've been most helpful," Buchholz replied sarcastically.

"Thank you for choosing Ace Lab Supplies," she said sweetly before disconnecting the line.

He dialed Wilson and gave him an update. "Bad news. The closest cadaver is in Cleveland. Apparently, you *couldn't* throw a dead cat and hit anything in Detroit because they are woefully short in supply."

"Are you sure? That pushes the timeline well beyond the window," Wilson stated.

"I've called six places already, and Ohio is our best option," Buchholz reassured him. "At least you don't have to drive there," he griped. "I shouldn't be doing this gopher shit—that's why we have staff."

"You know why we can't do that on this one," Wilson responded, carefully stressing each word.

"I know, I know, I know," he rattled off and let off some steam. He wasn't thrilled about tangling with Hor-Nebwy so soon after being free of him, but an order is an order. Plus, the vindictive part of him took pleasure that the old bastard was getting the shaft. Serves the mummy right for using his body like a puppet. "It's still annoying as hell."

"Have you told Leader yet?" Something in Wilson's voice piqued his interest.

"No. Why?"

"I have an idea. Give me the address and hang tight for ten minutes," Wilson offered.

"Is this going to get me in trouble?" Buchholz asked once he relayed the information.

"You wanna drive to Cleveland?" Wilson asked rhetorically.

Buchholz retracted his objection and signed off, "Hey, it's your ass on the line. We'll do this your way."

Wilson sat at his kitchen table looking at the remains of his breakfast—he was astounded at what could be delivered when he was willing to open the wards. It was mutually decided that he and Mau should keep a low profile until the Hor-Nebwy situation was resolved, but making the ancient mummy wait even longer carried its own dangers. Weighing the risks, he made an executive decision and called out with his thoughts. *Mau, could you come here?*

The cat blinked into existence in front of him. *You have no mice in this house*, she complained. She'd remembered the mortal realm as being one infested with vermin.

"I know. I'm sorry, you'll have to hunt outside," Wilson apologized aloud. "I have something I need you to do." He wasn't exactly sure of the parameters of their relationship. She wasn't his cat, but she did gain sentience by swallowing some of his soul. They were forever linked but neither was master over the other, although Wilson knew better than to say that to Mau directly.

Mau jumped onto the table and sat back on her haunches. She gave him the air of "I'm listening."

"You know how we made a plan to make sure I don't get killed?" he skirted around the request. The cat nodded. "Well, we've hit a snag and there's something I need you to get for us. I wouldn't ask, except we're already late."

Mau batted the request around like a stuffed toy before answering Crawling Shadow. *What do you want me to retrieve?*

*****

Buchholz drummed his fingers on his office desk. He didn't usually spend much time in the Salt Mine, just long enough to file his reports and expenses. Having so much rock between him and the sun put him on edge, and he hated that there was no wifi or internet there. Without his games to distract him, ten minutes stretched into an eternity, and he was trying to figure out if it was weird that he thought of salt as rock when he was in the Mine or if was weirder that he thought of it as food when he was outside of the Mine when someone knocked at his door.

"Come in," he called out before remembering the palm locks that prevented entry. He was halfway out of his chair when a massive black cat, carrying a wide-eyed Wilson by the scruff of his neck, appeared opposite his desk. Wilson was holding a hermetically sealed dead cat. Mau dropped Wilson and shrank back to normal size.

Buchholz fell back into his chair. "Well, I did say come in, didn't I?" He looked Wilson up and down. He was almost unrecognizable with the long hair and bushy beard, but the eyes were the same. He was wearing a suit, but it hung on his frame. He hadn't realized how muscular Wilson had been until it was gone. "You look like shit."

Wilson composed himself—he *would not* recommend travel by cat. "Thanks, I was trapped between realities. What's your excuse?" he jabbed back.

Hobgoblin was not expecting the verbal sparring from Wilson, whose most frequent talking point was "cut the nonessential chatter" when they worked together. "My beauty sleep was rudely interrupted," Buchholz retorted with a friendly grin and he bent down to pet Mau. "You're looking less desiccated than when I last saw you." Mau purred at the Hobgoblin's touch—he had freed her from the control of the Vengeful One.

"This all you need?" Wilson handed him the package.

"That's it. Chloe and Dot have everything else ready in the library," Buchholz confirmed. He pressed the button on the intercom and requested an escort. "It's Hobgoblin with Fulcrum and Kitty. We're ready to rock."

Buchholz jumped from his chair and grabbed his gear. "Let take care of it then, shall we?" he said gallantly as he opened the door. Mau followed the pair, albeit at her own languid pace.

They heard the elevator doors ping open by the time they were descending the ramp into the black and white common room. After a few seconds of holding the door, Dot impatiently called from the elevator, "Hurry up!"

"Coming!" Wilson yelled back. As they neared the doors, he described what an elevator was to Mau—he didn't want her freaking out in constrained quarters. He knew Mau could have just blinked there, but it was important to teach her manners and protocol—knock before entering, travel like a cat when you could, and only speak aloud when absolutely necessary. Blending in was essential if she didn't want Hor-Nebwy to catch wind of her escape.

She said nothing during his explanation but gave it a cautious sniff before crossing the threshold. Once inside, she spent most of it popping in and out of existence, each time appearing slightly above the space she'd just left. She thrilled at the purely mechanical movement.

The entourage followed the twins to one of Weber's extra rooms with plenty of table space and more importantly, a drain. The body of Arthur was laid out and atop the corpse was his sword, wrapped in the dirty tunics of Avalon and tied with the belts of its dead. Next to the sink sat a plastic bucket, a pair of scissors, a box of latex gloves, and a ratty towel.

Buchholz donned the gloves, opened the plastic bag containing the dead cat, and drained the excess liquid into the bucket. It stank and he felt bad for introducing this level of funk into Weber's domain. He held the cat over the bucket as Wilson daubed it with the towel, drying it as much as they could.

"Mau, could you remind Hobgoblin what you look like when you're resting?" Wilson asked aloud. The cat circled a few times, curled up on the floor, and turned into a mummy.

"Got it," Buchholz said. He opened his fish amulet and sucked in the dead cat as Mau changed back. "Everyone ready for the return?" he checked. The group readied their weapons and wills—sometimes the return trip could be bumpy.

Buchholz opened the amulet, and a perfect match of mummy Mau came out. Chloe shuttered. "No matter how many times I see that, it's still creepy."

"What do you think, Mau?" Wilson asked.

The cat sniffed and licked, rubbing her scent on it. She looked up and spoke, "The Hobgoblin tricks."

"Excellent!" Wilson beamed. If Mau said it was good, it's good. He turned to Hobgoblin. "Now do me."

"You're cute and all, but not really my type," Buchholz quipped.

Wilson smirked. "You should be so lucky to tap this ass. Now open the amulet, Hobgoblin."

Buchholz grinned—he could get used to this Wilson. He held the thought of Wilson in his mind and pulled out the closest corpse to his height and build. When the amulet opened again, a perfect match of Wilson fell out.

Wilson dressed it with care, covering the corpse with the ratty tunics he'd saved from his own return from Avalon. Preparing his own corpse felt weird, but it would have been stranger to watch someone else do it. "That should be it," he said with finality. Wilson reached down and stroked the center of Mau's head. "Are you ready for your last trip to the Valley of the Magi?"

"Meow," she answered and licked his hand.

"See you soon," he reassured her. She grew in size, large enough to carry everything in her mouth, and blinked out of sight.

*****

Hor-Nebwy felt a tug on the magical tripwire he had in place to alert him to Mau's return. *Finally!* he thought to himself. Even though she was a vehicle for him to exert his will, she was still a cat, which meant she was capricious with her concept of timeliness. He put down his tools and moved to his tomb in a single step. He wasn't against walking the length of his valley, but today was special. It was the day he could add the greatest of Avalon's treasures to his valley.

Mau was already in her mummified form when he arrived, curled and resting on top of his canopic chest as she always was. He petted the linen-wrapped bundle out of habit, but it was what she'd left on the ground that captured his attention—not one, but two corpses. Hor-Nebwy turned his sight on them and distinguished Arthur as the one with the sword. Its gold and ivory hilt was lost on the mummy's sightless eyes, but his other senses told him it was a thing of beauty. It was only right that a king be buried with his things, and the sword reeked of Arthur.

The second body Hor-Nebwy recognized as the petitioner who had struck the deal. His impatience with Mau dissipated once he pieced together the cause of her delay—her transient master had not the strength to leave Avalon, and she could only return to her true master once he had perished. The mummy swelled with pride at saving the most sacred treasure of Avalon despite the odds, and was moved to pity for the poor mortal. The bargain maker may not be worthy of one of Hor-Nebwy's tombs, but he was faithful in fulfilling his oath and such a deed demanded a minor honor, at the very least. He gathered his will, and the valley obeyed his command. A wave of sand rushed into the tomb, lifted the lowly corpse, and carried it to the sea of sand where it would forever rest beneath the dunes.

"Be at eternal peace in the valley," he solemnly spoke as a brief benediction before giving the gem of Avalon his full regard. Hor-Nebwy started a funerary song, extolling the deeds of Arthur as he escorted the body into the tomb he'd prepared especially for him. He removed the tattered tunics and systematically extracted the internal organs, placing each in its own canopic jar. Then he blew sand across the body, wicking out every last drop of moisture from it before wrapping it in linen. He unsheathed the sword and gave it a place of pride as the only possession of Arthur's that had escaped Avalon with him.

Hor-Nebwy finished his song, extinguished the flame of his clay oil lamp, and left Arthur to his final and eternal peace.

Time would pass, but Arthur would never end.

Epilogue

Leader's soft-soled shoes made little noise against the salt floor as she walked through the stacks of books toward the central desk in the Salt Mine's library. Chloe and Dot were waiting.

"Ready?" she asked.

The twins nodded in unison and hoisted the long, thin lead case from the floor. Dot grunted as she parked it on the table while Chloe kept her composure despite the effort. It was heavy for its size and covered with runes carefully crafted ages ago, with a few recent additions courtesy of the librarians.

"Do you want to take a peek before we put it to bed?" Chloe asked Leader.

"You won't regret it," Dot backed her sister.

Leader smiled. "Just a quick look," she agreed. The twins lowered the sealing ward and Leader lifted a corner of the lid. It was magnificent, gleaming under her perceptive eye. It called to her like a siren's song, beckoning her to wield it. She calmly closed the lid and motioned for the twins to seal it back up.

They distributed the weight between their six arms as best

they could and started for the elevators. "Do you think Hor-Nebwy will notice?" Chloe asked once they were headed deeper into the Salt Mine.

"I doubt it. He's got the real Arthur, which is what he really wanted. The sword is more tomb accoutrement than valued relic to someone like Hor-Nebwy," Leader posited. "The important thing is the sword we sent will still read as Arthur's on examination."

"Trading Clarent for Excalibur is worth the risk," Dot put in her two cents. "Even with all the extra wards we had to put on the case." If Leader had her druthers, the Salt Mine would be in possession of both, but concessions had to be made to keep Wilson and Mau in action; between the two, the sword in the stone would play second fiddle to the sword forged by Viviane and her sisters every time.

They exited on one of the many storage levels of the mine, passing through a series of warded thresholds until they reached their destination. The final door had an unremarkable plastic label bearing the words "Hard Lightning," and within the small room was a deepened ledge. They slid the case into the nook and covered it with the excavated salt.

They said nothing until they were back on the elevator, going up to the library. "Do you think Wilson knows what he is?" Dot asked Leader. The twins watched her for any sign or tell.

"Not yet, but he will eventually," she responded neutrally.

"And how's that going to work out?" Chloe inquired.

"We'll all keep an eye on him and watch closely," Leader answered reassuringly—she knew the twins liked him for all his peccadilloes. "Wilson's always been dedicated. I don't think that's going to change."

Chloe threw her sister a look of "I told you so," and Dot was happy to be wrong on this occasion. "I don't know. He invited us over for pizza and has a cat now. You think you know a guy," Dot scoffed.

"Indeed," Leader got the last word as the elevator came to a stop.

THE END

The agents of The Salt Mine will return in *Hen Pecked*

Printed in Great Britain
by Amazon

67217737R00121